THE WILL OF THE STANDING STONES

A HAMMOND & CIRCLE MYSTERY

AG BARNETT

ODDMOOR PRESS

FREE B**OO**K

Claim your free book by signing up to AG Barnett's
mailing list at agbarnett.com

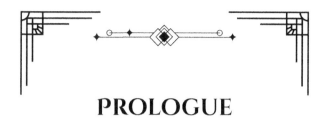

PROLOGUE

Elina Fortesque clutched the small red handbag to her side as she walked through the park in the fading light. Her heels echoed on the stone path and reverberated until suffocated into silence by the surrounding trees towering on either side of her.

She'd had another little windfall. Another lump sum to pay next month's rent and maybe give her some breathing space. She knew it wouldn't, though. She had said this the last time, yet her rent had still gone unpaid. Only her fluttering eyelashes and aristocratic accent had persuaded her leering landlord. She was good for it.

She knew her weaknesses well enough. There

was always another nightclub opening, another cocktail to try. She had lived her brief life up to this point as she pleased, and she wasn't about to change now, no matter what her father said. Yes, he had cut off her allowance, but she was intelligent enough to have found other ways of getting by.

She turned her head at the sound of a twig cracking to her right. She slowed as she peered into the small clump of trees, but saw nothing. Subconsciously, she picked up her pace as she ran through the list of places that were now off limits to her, due to bar bills. She would need to persuade the gang to try somewhere new tonight. Maybe Geronimo's, a new jazz club she had heard mentioned the other night.

She had almost reached the end of the section of path that was crowded by trees, and her pace quickened slightly.

A figure stepped out in front of her, making her gasp and rock back on her heels before the right-hand side of their face lit in a dull yellow glow from a nearby streetlamp.

She exhaled sharply before speaking. "Goodness! You scared me half to death! What on earth are you doing here?!"

The figure gave a small smile and moved towards her, but said nothing.

"Listen, I need to get back," Elina began, pausing when she saw the length of pipe in the figure's hand. She opened her mouth to shout, to scream, anything, but the noise stuck in her throat as the pipe swung down towards her head, and she fell into an endless darkness.

S tepping off the train at Moreton-in-Marsh train station, Flo Hammond made her way to the far side of the bustling platform. She turned to watch the porter pulling her suitcase down as the steam from the shuddering engine whirled and drifted around his feet. She had always loved that particular smell of a train running hot. She associated it with adventure. Something, she felt, she was all too lacking in her life.

She was deciding whether she had time for a cup of tea and maybe even a slice of cake at one of the many cafés she knew the town possessed, when she heard her name being called from behind her.

She turned to see Henry Bitten, his slick, black hair shining in the bright winter sun, with his hand raised in a wave. His bright blue eyes sparkled as he beamed at her. He was a dark and brooding kind of handsome, which utterly changed when he smiled, turning to a more mischievous, boyish charm. She noticed he still wore his old military belt from the war and felt the familiar pang she always did went that fresh scar on history came to mind. Just yesterday the unknown soldier had been buried at Westminster Abbey, representing all those who had fallen in the Great War.

She shook herself free from these glum recollections and focused on Henry.

When they'd first met, she was quite attracted to him, but of course, his attention was drawn to Elina. Since then, he had become more of a wayward brother to her.

She smiled back at him and waited for him to catch up with her.

"Henry!" she exclaimed as he reached her. "What on earth are you doing here?"

"I was going to ask you the same thing!" he said, taking her hands in his. "It's been too long," he added, looking into her eyes.

A prickling chill rose to the back of her neck as she thought back to when she had last seen him, at a graveside, in the rain.

"Yes, well," she said, pulling her hands away and clasping them in front of her, "I've been rather busy."

"Of course," Henry said, his expression turning somber before quickly returning to his wide smile.

"Guess who I ran into on the train?" He turned and looked back down the platform. There, a figure was struggling with two large suitcases. Emerging through the steam like some giant-handed monster.

"I had to leave him with the luggage, poor chap, but I saw you and wanted to catch you before you disappeared."

"George!" Flo said with delight as she recognised the approaching man.

"Hello Flo," George Wilson said, dropping the two suitcases down with a thump before shooting a quick scowl at Henry. "Good to see you."

He swept his blond hair back from his face and gave her an awkward grin. *Awkward* was a good word to describe George in general really, Flo thought.

"It's good to see you too." Flo smiled at him as

he pushed his thick-rimmed glasses back up his narrow nose. "Shall we go and grab some tea and catch up?"

"Oh," George said, his face falling. "I'm afraid I've booked a car to take me on from here."

"And I'm going to catch a ride," Henry added. "It turns out Henry and I are heading to the same place. Long Barrow, wherever that is."

Flo gasped, her hand moving to her mouth.

"But that's extraordinary! That's where I'm heading too!"

"Wait," Henry said, reaching into his jacket pocket and pulling a somewhat battered letter from his inside pocket. "Did you get one of these as well? An invitation to a reading of a will?"

"Yes!" Flo said in astonishment, "Though I've no idea who this Mr Badala is."

"Neither do we," Henry said, gesturing to George.

"You got one too?" Flo looked at him.

"Yes, all rather curious, isn't it?" George said in his quiet voice. "There's room in the car, though. We can all go over together. We're booked into the Red Lion there for tonight."

"Me too!" Flo laughed. "Not that there was much choice, of course. Well," she said, smiling at them both and placing her hands on her hips. "The old gang back together again, eh? Well, almost." Her smile faded and her lips pursed.

" Oh, come on," Henry said, "let's not go over all that now. We're back together and part of a mystery inheritance, apparently! Let's enjoy it. "

"You're right," Flo said. "Come on then, one of you can carry my suitcase."

"George is your man there," Henry said, picking up his own case in his right hand and linking his left through Flo's, guiding her down the high street.

George sighed and picked up his case and Flo's before following them.

CHAPTER

TWO

Anna Buckley stood at the discoloured window of the small bedroom and looked out at the street below. Three young people were entering the inn where she and her husband were staying. She pursed her lips. Her own youth seemed to slip away ever faster these days.

She turned away from the window and looked at her husband, Edward. His stocky frame wedged into a chair at the desk in the corner of the room. The *Times* newspaper opened in front of his head, obscuring his jowled face and bristling moustache.

His youth, of course, had already been left far behind. Although only ten years older than her at fifty-two, since his semi-retirement, he had settled into being an old man with relish. All he required to be happy these days was his pipe, a good meal, and a drink never far from his hand.

"Really Edward, must we stay in such a..." She struggled to find a word which described her distaste of the Red Lion inn's faded nature. "In such a provincial inn."

She knew the place wasn't that bad. She was sure that at some point it had been a very respectable establishment. Now, though, it had faded into... not disrepair, but despair. A sad fading of fabric and scuffing of furniture that showed it had seen better days. With a pang of annoyance and horror, she realised it was, in fact, the perfect place for them.

"You know we had no choice, dear," Edward answered distractedly.

She hated not having his full attention.

She moved across to him and pulled the paper down with her pale finger. "Are you sure this inheritance business isn't some kind of trick in order to uncover your dirty little secret?"

She watched his moustache twitch and his cheeks redden.

"Really Anna, I wish you would let it go."

Let it go? How could she? It was her driving and pushing his naturally lazy self that had taken them up in the world, and it was his incompetence that had taken them down. Their reputation wasn't entirely ruined, but the social invitations they received had declined in quality. Why was the fall from grace so much easier than the climb to get there?

What could she do, though? Edward had been her escape from her old life in the country. A life of hard work and drudgery. Where the farm had sucked the hours and days from her family like a starving leech.

She exhaled slowly and leaned down, smiling at him as she reached out her hand to hold the side of his face. "You did what you had to do," she whispered.

She watched his features soften and then pulled her hand away and moved back to the window. She stared out at the darkening grey sky for a moment before speaking in a low tone.

"That doesn't mean the past isn't stalking you."

THREE

K ate Fielding waited until she heard the gentle splashing of her employer lowering herself into the bath, before hurrying across to the window and pulling the typed letter from the pocket of her apron.

Her hands shook as she read through the few scant lines of text for what must have been the hundredth time. Certain phrases jumping out at her, 'inheritance' and 'to your significant advantage.' She didn't understand it, couldn't understand it. None of it made any sense.

She moved back to the bathroom and listened at the door for a moment, making sure the future Lady Baxter was still bathing, before heading to the desk in the room's corner. Lifting the flap on the envelope that was resting there, she pulled out the letter from inside and held it alongside hers breathlessly, as she had done before. The letters were identical. Someone had left both her and her employer an inheritance, the same person.

Surely it must be some kind of mistake? Or perhaps, just perhaps, it was a chance for her to escape.

Or could it be just part of the tightening prison she had found herself in for the last six months?

She returned both letters to their places, closed her eyes and took in three long breaths to calm herself.

"Kate," her mistress called through the door.

She steeled herself and headed for the bathroom.

CHAPTER

FOUR

Flo, Henry and George looked down at the three typewritten letters laid out on the table before them. Each letter had used exactly the same wording, written with identical spacing and form.

"Maybe it was some old chap we met in London one time and have forgotten about? You know the sort. Rich old types having a secret last hurrah while the wife's off visiting her sick sister or something. I'm sure I've met a hundred ancient old fossils about town, and I can't remember any of them. They all just blend into one above a certain age, don't you think?" Henry said.

"Don't you think that we'd remember them if

all three of us had made such an impression that they named us in their will?" Flo said.

"You don't think," George began, then paused as the eyes of the others turned to him. He swallowed hard before continuing. "You don't think it has anything to do with Elina, do you?"

"Don't be stupid, George," Henry said, "it's got nothing to do with all that."

Flo sipped at her gin and tonic, her eyes turning to the open archway that led through to the main bar area of the Red Lion pub in Long Compton.

She had tried so hard to move on over the last six months. She had even tried to forget those fantastic, wild and free days they had all enjoyed in London, because it was all too hard now. Too painful. And now they were back together—well, not all of them.

She knew someone was staring at her. A dark-eyed, curvaceous woman with a disordered black bob was eyeing her over a golden-coloured cocktail from the bar.

As the woman caught her eye, she smiled, rose from her stool and headed towards the side room where Flo and the others sat. She was dressed in all black, and with a slight, envious thrill, Flo saw she was wearing trousers. She had never been so bold as to wear them herself.

"I'm sorry for staring at you," the woman said in an American accent, "but I just heard the most fascinating story and I couldn't help but be intrigued. Jesse Circle," she said, offering her hand towards Flo, who shook it in a slightly dazed manner.

Close up, the woman was a lot to take in. She had sharp cheekbones which were softened by the roundness of her face. Her pale skin contrasted, in Flo's mind, rather brazenly with her bright, blood-red lipstick. Similar in years to Flo, she had a lively, vivacious face that intrigued Flo immediately.

Unlike Flo's flat and shapeless frame, Jessie was curvaceous to the point of salaciousness.

"I'm Flo Hammond, this is George Wilson and Henry Bitten."

"Very nice to meet you all," Jesse said, shaking each of their hands vigorously.

"So what was the story you heard?" Henry asked, a playful glint in his eye.

"May I join you?" Jesse said, pulling a chair from a nearby table and sitting down without waiting for an answer.

"First, this is a place full of stories. The people

here talk about witches as though the skies were teeming with broomsticks every night. Then you have the standing stones."

"Stones?" George asked.

"Yes, ancient pagan monuments. You know, like Stonehenge. There's a circle of these stones near here, thousands of years old. The story goes like this." She leaned forward in her seat and placed her elbows on the table.

She had a punchy sort of rhythm to her speech that Flo found utterly engaging, and her American accent felt wildly exotic in this rural English setting.

"The story goes that there was a healer in these parts who tended to the sick in all the local villages. One day, a child was too sick and the woman could do nothing to save her. The bitterness over her death lead to rumours spreading and soon the healer was being vilified as a witch. The locals decided she was, in fact, the one making people sick. One day, the healer invited the leaders of the surrounding villages to meet with her, where she said she would give them all a magnificent gift to repay them for the trouble she had caused. When they arrived, she turned them all to stone, and that's the circle that still stands today!" She sat back with a wide smile.

Henry snorted with laughter. "What a load of old nonsense."

"Ah," Jessie said, "I see you're the cynical sort, Henry?"

"I am when it comes to witches and men being turned to stone."

"And what about you, George?" Jessie said, turning to him.

"Oh, I don't know." He smiled shyly.

"Don't bother asking George." Henry laughed. "He can never decide what he thinks about anything."

"Well, I think it's a fine story," Flo said determinedly. "I'd like to see these stones."

"Well, I'm sure you'll get your chance with where you're heading," Jessie said.

There was a momentary pause as the other three exchanged glances.

"Are you going to Standings House as well? You received a letter?" Flo asked.

Jessie smiled. "No, I didn't receive a letter, but you all did, I assume? I find it very interesting."

"It's strange is what it is," George said with a

frown. "I can't help the feeling that the whole thing is some kind of joke."

"Oh, come on," Henry said with derision, "it would be elaborate as a joke, don't you think? You hear about these kinds of things. You know, some old relative you didn't know you had has keeled over and left you a wad of cash."

"Yes," George said rather wearily, "but if that was the case, they would hardly have left something to all three of us, would they?"

"I assume the three of you are not related?" Jessie said as she swirled her drink.

"No," Flo answered with a shake of her head.

Jessie studied them for a moment, and Flo had the unnerving sensation that they were being judged.

"You're not the only ones to receive a letter, you know," Jessie continued, her eyes searching each of them.

"I thought you said you didn't get one?" Henry said.

"I didn't, but there are at least two other guests staying here at the moment who did."

"How extraordinary," George said in an awed whisper. "What were their names?"

"A Mr and Mrs Buckley, according to the bartender."

"Buckley?" George asked.

"Yes," Jessie said quizzically, "do you know them?"

George gave a small, shy laugh.

"Sorry, no. I just keep hoping to find a name I'm familiar with in this, so it makes sense."

"They were asking the bartender about the setup at Standings House."

"What do you know about it?" Flo asked eagerly, "What can you tell us?"

Jessie leaned back and smiled. Her shining eyes matching the slate grey sky which dominated the window behind her.

"Well, this is where things get really interesting," she said before rising from her seat. "But first, I think I'd like to treat you all to a round of drinks. There is a condition, though."

"What's that?" Flo laughed.

"I am determined to get the English drinking Bee's Knees if it kills me, so that's what you're all having." She swept off before any of them could say any more.

"What an extraordinary woman," Henry said, watching her leave.

"I think she's fantastic," Flo said, a note of wonder in her voice.

"This is all a bit fishy," George said. "Getting letters about a mysterious inheritance from someone none of us have ever heard of, and now we're in a village talking about witches with a woman wearing trousers."

"And what's wrong with a woman wearing trousers?" Flo asked him, one eyebrow raised.

"Oh, well, nothing, of course," George stammered in reply.

"It's just that you're stuck in the dark ages?" Henry offered with a sly smile.

"Who is?" Jessie said, arriving back at the table with a quizzical look.

"George here," Henry said.

"Nonsense," Jessie said firmly. "I'm sure George here is a man of progressive thought and action."

George immediately turned a deep scarlet, while Henry snorted with laughter.

"He's an accountant and I'm afraid if you cut through him like a stick of rock, he's accountant all the way through," Henry said as the bartender arrived with a tray of cocktails.

"I know you British rarely go in for table service in pubs," Jessie said, ignoring Henry's comments, "but David here is just adorable, aren't you, David?"

The ruddy-faced barman rubbed a hand across the back of his thick neck and chuckled as he retreated to the bar with the empty tray.

"Cheers," Jessie said, raising her glass to the others before taking a long sip of the amber-coloured liquid. The others picked up their glasses and looked slightly suspiciously at them.

"Oh, come on, it won't kill you." Jessie laughed.

The three of them took sips.

"That's delicious," Flo said, with the others nodding in agreement.

"Gin, honey and lemon," Jessie said. "Of course, I had to bring my own honey." She pulled a small jar from her handbag and waggled it at them before it vanished away again.

"Quaint, but English pubs never have any. Right, onto the interesting stuff." She leaned forward in a conspiratorial manner.

"Standings House is just a few miles down the road at the bottom of the valley. It's owned by one of the Oxford University colleges, but someone has recently rented it." She raised her eyebrows expectantly.

"Why would they hire an entire house just to invite people for a will reading?" Flo asked.

"That's a good question," Jessie said, pointing a finger at her, causing the multiple bracelets she wore to jangle. "Seems a strange thing to do, right?"

"What on earth?" George said..

"It makes little sense," Henry added, shaking his head. "A law firm just wouldn't do that, surely?"

"Unless instructed to in the will?" Flo said. "Maybe this Mr Badala had some connection with the place and wanted his will read there and the money is coming from his estate?"

Jessie laughed a loud, braying laugh that made Flo jump. It was a noise closer to that a donkey would make than one expected of the elegant and sophisticated American in front of her.

"You have a good, enquiring mind, Flo!" Jessie said to her. "I was never very good at asking the right questions. I'm better at sniffing out trouble than resolving it."

"Flo here is a crime reporter," Henry said with a grin.

"Oh! How fantastic!" Jessie responded with glee.

"Hardly," Flo said, somewhat embarrassed. "I actually write a women's interest column for the *Standard*, but last year I happened upon a murder case and wrote it up. Of course, they published it under a pseudonym."

Jessie raised one eyebrow. "A male one, no doubt?"

Flo nodded as they shared a look that women so often did and wished they didn't have to.

"In any case," Flo said, "it appears we have a bit of a mystery of our own here. Though I'm sure there's a simple explanation that we'll find out in good time."

"I have to admit," Jessie said, "I had the same thoughts when I heard it from the bartender. I thought it was nothing more than a slightly over-the-top and theatrical will reading. That was until I heard the Buckleys have not heard of the Mr Badala whose will was being read. That struck me as curious. Now, the three of you appear with the same story... well, come on!" She slapped the table for emphasis. "You can't help but think something fishy is going on."

Flo's gaze lifted and became unfocused for a

moment. "Then, of course," she said slowly, "there's the name."

"The name?" Henry asked. "You mean, Standings House? It is a strange name."

Flo snapped back into focus with a smile.

"Yes, of course. The house," Flo said with a smile.

Jessie continued, "Well, that's just one more intriguing thing about this place and what's happening, isn't it? The standing stones."

"I don't see what relevance some old wives' tale has?" Henry asked.

"Don't you think it's interesting?" Jessie said. "Someone lures people into a trap and then turns them all to stone." She looked between the three of them.

"You think we're being lured into a trap?" Henry said, laughing. "Though I think I'd make a fine statue." He turned his head to the side and upwards in a mock pose.

Jessie stared at him, her eyes sparkling.

"Well, I, for one, hope so."

"You want it to be a trap?" Flo asked, confused.

"Well, don't you think that would be so exciting?!"

"Have you ever heard the phrase, 'careful what you wish for'?" Flo replied.

"Can't say I have." Jessie grinned. "It must be an English term. Cheers!"

She clinked her glass heavily against Flo's and drained the remaining liquid.

CHAPTER

FIVE

"Good evening... Mr Hove," the man said.

He watched the strange figure give a small bow before walking away into the night and opened the envelope he had been handed, his thumb flicking through the money inside as he smiled.

He slipped the envelope into his jacket pocket and turned to look back at the Red Lion Inn. It was better to not ask questions. He'd learned that the hard way in his younger days, but he couldn't help it in this case. Just what on earth was this all about?

At least he had his first instructions now. He looked at the typed sheets in his hand.

30

'Read them, memorise them, and then burn them,' the man had said. Why all this secrecy?

He scanned through the first few lines of text.

This was going to be interesting....

CHAPTER

SIX

Flo looked in the mirror as she applied her lipstick and frowned. It certainly wasn't the fiery red of Jessie Circle's lipstick. She sighed. What she would give to have even a tenth of the bold confidence the American had shown.

CHAPTER

SEVEN

Outside Flo's room, George Wilson straightened his tie before raising his hand to knock.

"Morning, old boy," a voice called out down the hallway.

He turned to see Henry approaching with his wide, handsome grin, and his stomach fell.

"Morning, Henry," he said coldly.

Henry Bitten, he thought. Everything had been fine until he had arrived a year ago. It had just been him and Flo and Elina. The thought of Elina swiftly brought his annoyance into sadness. He gestured to the door.

"I was just calling on Flo to go down to breakfast," he said.

"Capital idea." Henry grinned as he rapped on the door.

George grimaced as he turned back to the door, but as it opened, he couldn't help but break into a wide smile.

"Morning!" Flo said, her round blue eyes as bright and clear as ever.

George felt his chest tighten, as it always did when he saw her, and as it had only done occasionally over the past six months.

"Are we ready to discover what fate has in store for us?' she said in her ever chirpy tones.

"You make it sound so dramatic," Henry said with a laugh.

"Oh, come on, we're going to a mysterious house for some inheritance from a mysterious benefactor. It's the most exciting thing that's..." She halted, the light in her face dimming as her skin paled.

"It's OK," George said, reaching out and putting one hand on her arm. She looked up, smiled at him, and he jerked his hand away as though something had electrocuted him.

"Shall we go down to breakfast?" he said as his cheeks flushed.

"Absolutely," Flo answered, "I'm famished."

"Morning!" A voice rang down the hallway towards them.

They turned to see Jessie Circle wearing a sharply cut tweed jacket and what looked like riding jodhpurs, and advancing towards them with long, purposeful strides.

"Heading down to breakfast? I wonder if I could just borrow you a moment, Flo?" A flurry of movement accompanied the torrent of words as she pushed through George and Henry to place a long arm around Flo.

"Oh, yes, of course," Flo said, slightly flustered.

"We'll meet you chaps downstairs in just a moment," Jessie continued. "This is your room, is it?" she asked, turning to the door behind Flo and pushing it open.

Flo gave the others a shrug and a grin that firmly suggested 'Americans. What can you do?' before following her in.

"I hope you don't mind me tearing you away from your very exciting love triangle, but I'm afraid I need a favour."

"Love triangle?!" Flo cried, then put her hand to her mouth and repeated it in a hissed whisper, "Love triangle?!"

"Oh," Jessie said, tilting her head to one side

for a moment before shaking it. "Apologies. Let's talk about this favour. I wonder if I could come with you to Standings House today, as a companion? I'm sure no one will think it strange that you would bring a friend when travelling." She frowned. "In fact, it's a little strange you didn't, frankly." Her grey eyes fixed Flo with an intense stare.

"I—" Flo began, before she felt the familiar weight of sadness rising in her chest. "I don't have many friends," she finished weakly.

"Nonsense! A girl like you?" Jessie dismissed the idea with a wave of her hand as she moved across the window. "Anyway, to be completely honest, I have this terrible affliction, cursed with it since birth. No doubt inherited from one of my parents, maybe both. Who knows? I don't know who they were. It's totally incurable."

"An affliction?" Flo said, trying to follow this strange, fast-paced and one-sided conversation.

"Curiosity," Jessie said, her eyes shining with a devilish sparkle. "I'm absolutely cursed with it, that and an outright allergic reaction to boredom. So how about it?"

Flo looked at the extraordinary force of nature in front of her and decided that she very much wanted to spend more time in her company.

"Yes, of course! It will be lovely to have someone with me. I don't mind admitting that this whole thing has given me," she paused and gave a shy smile, "well, to use an American phrase, the heebie-jeebies."

"Yes," Jessie said, her manner suddenly slow and serious. "I noticed that last night. Of course, it does seem a very peculiar situation," she shrugged, "that's why I'm interested. There's something else there, though, something hanging over the three of you. You're friends clearly, but I feel something has come between you somehow?"

"My friend," Flo said, and already she could feel the tears gathering in her eyes. "She died six months ago. I... I found it very hard."

Jessie strode across the room to her and embraced her.

The unexpected gesture shocked Flo too much to do anything other than accept it. After a silent moment, Jessie pulled back and looked at her, her hands on her arms.

"I'm very sorry to hear that, Flo." She turned and walked back to the window, which looked down into the street below.

"I can see why you find this whole situation unsettling. The three of you invited to this reading after a friend died, it's all very...," she turned back to Flo with a smile, "interesting." The smile faded slightly. "I'm afraid I can't help feeling that something is terribly wrong here. From the moment I heard what was happening this weekend from the bartender last night, I've felt there is a hint of something tragic about the whole thing."

Flo opened her mouth and then closed it again, unsure of what to say.

"Anyway," Jessie said, brightening again as though the dark shadow that seemed to have fallen across them had passed. "You'll have me with you, so no worries there. Now, shall we join your two gentlemen at breakfast?"

She took Flo's arm and led her out into the corridor where they paused, letting a tall, strikingly beautiful woman pass, with a short, dumpy maid in tow.

They smiled at her, but she turned her eyes away from them as she strode down the hallway.

"Now," Jessie said in a whisper. "Who do you suppose she is?"

"I don't have a clue," Flo answered.

"Oh, come on, let's try to determine some sense of the woman from what we've seen."

"How do you mean?"

"Make some assumptions."

"OK...," Flo said, frowning at the now empty corridor where the woman had vanished from. "Expensive dress and wrap, showy for breakfast at a country inn. In fact, she doesn't seem to fit here at all." She paused thoughtfully. "I wouldn't be surprised if we welcomed another guest for the will reading," Flo said.

"Flo!" Jessie exclaimed, "You're an absolute marvel!"

"Do you think so?" Flo frowned, slightly amazed at her own train of thought, and also at the idea that this small inn seemed packed with people attending the same mysterious event as she was.

"And the maid," Flo found herself saying.

"The maid?" Jessie said, her brow furrowing.

"You see a glamorous woman," Flo continued, "and your gaze is naturally drawn to her, but one must always look at the servants. Sometimes you can catch a glimpse of what they really think about their employer, or maybe how the mood in their household truly is compared to the show their employers put on. That maid, for instance, is in absolute terror of something or someone."

Jessie looked at her in surprise, stopping in the corridor as Flo felt her cheeks flush.

"I'm sorry, I'm sure it's nothing," she said hurriedly and continued on without looking back.

They reached the breakfast room, where a shy young girl greeted them.

"Are you in Mr Badala's party?" she squeaked in a thick, country accent.

"Well, I've never heard of a dead man throwing a party before," Jessie laughed, "but yes, we are."

The young girl blushed and curtsied for some unknown reason before gesturing them to the back of the room.

"If you'd take a table at the back, Mr Hove will address the party, um, the group, shortly." She looked at them awkwardly for a moment and then, unsure what to do next, gave another small curtsy and bobbed away.

"Something tells me the Red Lion Inn isn't used to having large groups of salubrious guests to stay," Jessica said, taking Flo's arm once more. "Now then, not only are we going to get breakfast, I suspect we're about to meet our fellow players in this little game."

George and Henry were sitting at a table to their left. The tall, glamorous woman they had seen in the corridor was alone at a table on the right, her maid hovering awkwardly against the wall nearby as though trying to become part of the plasterwork. She was pale enough to be making a good fist of it.

At the middle table sat a couple. The man was a rotund figure with a ruddy complexion, his large moustache wriggling as he tucked into the bacon and eggs in front of him. His wife, if that's who she was, was a thin, birdlike woman who sipped at a black coffee, nose held high.

Jessie beamed at them all as she approached the table where George and Henry sat.

"Good morning all!" she said enthusiastically, making Flo wince. and attempt to give the room a look that said, 'I'm terribly sorry, but she's American and you know how they are.'

There was a mumbled good morning from the stout gentleman with the moustache in between mouthfuls, and no response from the two women, who returned a look that suggested small talk wasn't exactly on the menu.

"As we're all part of this exciting little party, we might as well acquaint ourselves, don't you think? My name is Jessie Circle, this is Flo Hammond, George Wilson and Henry Bitten."

"Circle?" the gruff male of the couple at the middle table said. "What sort of name is that?"

"Oh, I know!" Jessie laughed, "Isn't it too much?! I was an orphan and I'm afraid they had rather a curious humour when it came to giving the abandoned children names. Still, at least I wasn't as unfortunate as poor Billy Oblong!"

Flo gave a snort of laughter before flushing red and covering her mouth.

It wasn't just the comment, which she was sure was a joke, that had made her laugh. It was also the fact that Jessie was now talking in a perfect English accent.

"And what might your name be?" Jessie continued to the man.

"I'm Edward Buckley and this is my wife Anna."

"An absolute pleasure to meet you both!"

She faced the elegant woman who perched upright on her breakfast chair as though she were in an upmarket hotel cocktail bar.

"And you?"

The woman sat upright and lifted her chin

before answering in a clipped voice. "My name is Juliet Atoll."

Flo watched Jessie's smile widen.

"Is it really? Well, how wonderful, and you?" Jessie said, wheeling around to the nervous-looking maid, who was still standing against the wall.

"That is my maid," Juliet snapped, "and she should wait over by the door and not hover like some kind of bespectacled owl."

"Sorry, miss," the maid muttered before scurrying towards the door.

Flo watched Jessie frown after the retreating figure for a moment before turning back to the small gathering with a smile.

"Now, I guess we all sit and wait for the main event to start!" Jessie clapped her hands together, grabbed some toast from the silver rack on the table, and began buttering it enthusiastically.

"So then, chaps," Jessie said, her voice once again dripping with the American twang that, now more than ever, seemed so out of place in this small rural and very English dining room. "Have we missed anything?"

"Nothing," Henry said. "Apparently, some chap called Hove is going to come and talk to us all."

"Any idea who it is?" Flo asked.

"None," George replied. "Can I get you some toast?" He lifted the toast rack towards her, where the two remaining slices promptly fell out onto the table.

"You silly ass," Henry said, laughing.

"Sorry, sorry," George said as he replaced the toast and attempted to sweep up the crumbs. Jessie helped him as Flo's eyes scanned the room's occupants with interest.

"Funny sort of bunch we make, isn't it?" she said in a thoughtful whisper.

A tall, rangy man entered the room with his hands tucked in his waistcoat pockets, jacket pulled back to either side. His rather excitable features scanned the room with an air of importance that he didn't entirely pull off with his presence. His thin eyebrows matching his impossibly thin moustache, which clung to his top lip in two jet-black lines as though drawn on with coal.

"Good morning, ladies and gentlemen," he said with the smallest hint of a bow. "My name is Jonathan Hove and I have the honour of being the executor of Mr Badala's will, having served as his solicitor for many years." He paused, his bulging eyes scanning the room. "Mr Badala has several stipulations for the reading of this will, which might seem unusual. Believe me, though, when I say these small trifles are certainly worth a share of what is a considerable fortune."

There was nervous shuffling from the audience as people adjusted their seating position.

"What sort of stipulations?" barked Edward Buckley.

"Nothing too onerous... Mr Buckley, isn't it?"

Buckley made a small grunt of confirmation and Hove continued.

"In order to receive your share of the inheritance, you must come to the Standings estate as you already know, where you will stay for two nights."

"Two nights!" exclaimed Juliet Atoll.

"Correct, Miss Atoll," Hove continued with another small bow.

"Rest assured, your every comfort will be provided for. Those of you that have completed your task by Sunday lunchtime will receive your share of Mr Badala's fortune."

"Task? What task?" Henry said.

Flo turned to him and saw his handsome face pinched into a deep frown. There was a sort of tension in the room that hadn't been there before.

It was like the high whine of a discordant violin amidst an orchestra that, once noticed, was hard to ignore.

"All will be revealed in good time," Hove said. "Now please, enjoy your breakfast and a car will be sent to take you to Standings House in one hour, where there will be a small excursion to the local landmark."

F lo looked out her bedroom window at the hills which rose to the sky, blanketed in dark green trees. She gave a small shudder, unable to shake the feeling that she had descended to the bottom of some sort of pit.

Flo could see the standing stones from her bedroom window, even through the driving rain, set into one hill like a scar. Standings House was a large and creaky old place, filled with heavy furniture of dark wood and the faintest hint of mustiness emanating from its solid walls. Even the staff, from what she'd seen of them, seemed to reflect Flo's strange feeling of something not being quite right about the place. The butler that had greeted them at the front door sported a fearsome, dark

47

beard which looked as though it should belong to a much younger man. As if that wasn't enough of a feature to find on a butler, his swarthy, weather-beaten complexion, combined with a jet-black eye patch and slicked-back hair, gave him the air of a pirate. It was all Flo could do to not gape at the man as he'd instructed a skinny, rather simian-looking boy to carry their cases and shown them to their rooms.

The fires had at least been lit, and their heat battled against the icy air that hung around the draughty windows. A fight, Flo was sure, that would be lost in the night as the embers died down.

A loud rap on her bedroom door made her jump. She admonished herself for this jumpiness with a shake of the head as she moved to answer it.

"Isn't it amazing?" Jessie said as she burst through the door and into the room. "You can almost feel the years coming off the walls like steam! Of course," she laughed, "that could just be mould spores."

"It's definitely got character," Flo said as she closed the door.

Jessie snorted with laughter. "I forget how ridiculously polite the English can be."

Flo looked at her questioningly. "You seemed to put on a pretty good English accent at breakfast earlier."

Jessie smiled, her almond-shaped eyes sparkling with mischief as she answered in a perfect English accent.

"How do you know it's not the American accent that I'm putting on?"

Flo gaped at her.

"Are you telling me you're English?"

Jessie lifted herself up onto the dressing table where she perched, cross-legged, leaning back on her hands.

"I prefer to think of myself as a citizen of the world rather than any specific country." She shrugged, "Maybe because I was an orphan, I don't have weighty historical ties as most do."

"I'm sorry."

"Don't be," Jessie said lightly. "I was one of the lucky ones. A sweet old English lady who was living in New York adopted me. She was lonely and luckily for me, she also was kind, and filthy rich. I had to speak perfect English at home, but wanted to fit in the few times I escaped the house and got into town. I ended up being a sort of hybrid."

"You said, *was*—is she no longer with us?"

"She died, if that's what you mean. Then I had to leave America for, let's just say... reasons. Anyway, enough about me. What's your story?"

"Oh," Flo said, blinking. "Well, there's not much to tell, really. The youngest sister of four, my father calls himself a farmer, which upsets Mother terribly, but really we own a pretty insignificant bit of land in Sussex with tenants and things. I moved to London hoping to find something of my own, I think." She frowned at the well-worn and thinning carpet at her feet. "For a while I thought I had."

"And what happened?"

Flo looked up, her delicate face pinched in sorrow.

"I'm afraid I've been in a bit of a muddle since my friend died."

Jessie jumped for the dressing table and embraced her with such speed that Flo almost fell over backwards.

"Well, for the next couple of days on this adventure, let's not talk of it again. Afterwards, I will make it my sole aim to get you out of your muddle." She stood back, her hands on Flo's arms. "How does that sound?"

"That's very kind of you. You don't even know me."

"Strangers are just friends you haven't met yet," Jessie said, before throwing back her head with that braying laugh. "Listen to me sounding all profound! I must have read that before somewhere. It can't possibly be mine. It's far too witty. I've always found that it serves you well to remember the clever phrases of others when you're not blessed to make any of your own."

It was Flo's turn to laugh this time. There was something about her new acquaintance that made her feel as though she was always somehow behind in the conversation. Almost as though she was trying to eavesdrop on two people talking and only being able to make out some of it.

That said, she had enjoyed no one's company as much in some time.

"Shall we venture downstairs and see if that terrifying butler can point us in the gin's direction?" Jessie said, moving back towards the door.

Flo followed her automatically with a slightly dazed smile on her thin lips.

J uliet Atoll sat at the dressing table in her room, adjusting her hair absentmindedly in the mirror. The key was to not panic. There could be a perfectly reasonable explanation for him being here.

She just needed to pluck up the courage and do something she had been particularly avoiding recently: Talk to him.

There was a clatter from the bathroom as Kate dropped some toiletry or other. What on earth was wrong with her? As if her own nerves weren't on edge enough, her maid seemed to have lost hers completely. She'd been increasingly absent-minded over the last few months, but had turned into a gibbering wreck for the last few days. Not that she would say what was bothering her.

If she didn't snap out of it, she might have to be replaced.

Juliet sighed and looked down at the letter in front of her again. She had thought this might be a way out, a way for her to regain control of her life. Now? Now she didn't know what this strange weekend would bring, but the tension she had felt rise since this morning seemed to be wrapped around this gloomy house like a tourniquet. She wasn't sure what would happen when it was released.

"I don't see what you expect me to do about it?" Edward Buckley grumbled as he looked out of his bedroom window at the grounds of Standings House.

"I expect you to find out why we're here along with this strange and frankly alarming group of people," Anna answered coldly, trying not to think of the disturbing image of the butler who had sent a shiver down her spine when he had greeted them at the door.

"But I don't know any of these blighters! This Badala chap has obviously decided they're the ones to benefit from his estate, but what is that to us? As long as we get some tidy sum from the whole thing."

"And if we don't? Maybe we're an afterthought in this business. We must be able to establish a significant claim."

"We don't even know who the chap was!" Edward exclaimed.

"Then we must find out," Anna said simply. "Find out our connection to this Badala person and then discover all we can about our guests here and if there is any way that some of them might be ineligible to inherit."

Edward sighed as his eyes scanned the horizon of the hills which towered above the house. It was no use arguing with Anna when she was in this frame of mind. No use at all.

L unch had been a selection of cold meats, cheese and crusty bread arranged on the dining table for the guests to help themselves. The only oddity Flo had noticed was that they had set the table for nine, and not the eight which matched their party.

The group had largely stayed in its component parts, with the Buckleys and Juliet Atoll both ordering a selection of food to be taken to their rooms.

Flo, Jessie, George and Henry had eaten and then had drinks as they stared out of the tall French doors at the dull grey sky. They had chatted about the weather, and their strange situation until the butler, Stammerthwaite, had informed them that there would shortly be an excursion to the standing stones.

The small party donned the wrappings of winter as they gathered in the hallway, from the thick and luxurious fur coat of Juliet Atoll to the men's array of dark, thick wool coats and hats. The atmosphere was as frosty as the air outside that they were about to set forth into. There had been vigorous complaints from both the Buckleys and Juliet Atoll at the excursion to the standing stones, the weather being the overriding one. The wind was rising, and the air had turned bitter as it whipped against the old house with audibly increasing aggression.

Jonathan Hove, though, quelled the complaints by explaining that the excursion was a requirement for the inheritance, and anyone not taking part would be asked to leave and would give up any right to a claim. This had caused further murmurings of discontent, but to Flo's mild surprise, no one left.

"Now," Hove announced from the front of the hall. "If you could all kindly follow me, we can be on our way. Stammerthwaite will follow with warm refreshments for once we reach the circle."

He turned and opened the large door, which swung back violently in the wind.

As they followed him out into the grey light of the clouded late morning, Jessie touched Flo's shoulder.

"Won't be a moment," she said, before dashing off and talking to the dramatic-looking butler and then returning. She linked arms with Flo and pulled her towards the door.

"I have to say, Flo," she began, before Flo could ask what she had been doing, "that meeting you and being involved in this adventure is the most exciting thing that's happened to me in the two weeks I've been in this country. That's no idle compliment either. I've had an interesting two weeks."

Flo was about to ask why, when the conversation moved on again.

"It's strange, isn't it? What greed will do to people?"

"What do you mean?" Flo asked.

"Take Juliet Atoll. She's soon to become the Duchess of Grafton."

"The Duchess of Grafton!" Flo exclaimed.

"That's right. They made the announcement in the papers just last week. She had a rather fetching pearl necklace in the photograph, as I remember..."

Flo turned to her as her words trailed off.

Jessie had placed a cigarette in a holder and was now lighting it, with some difficulty in the blustery conditions.

"Anyway, here she is, trudging up a hill in winter to get a slice of a fortune from someone she doesn't know."

"Why bother, you mean?"

"That's exactly what I mean. I'm not too up on my dukes and duchesses, but from the look of her clothes, she will not want for anything. We can say the same of Mrs Buckley."

There were low voices and the sound of crockery clinking from behind them, and they turned to see Juliet Atoll's maid and the butler, Stammerthwaite, following with trays.

"I wonder why Juliet Atoll's maid is helping with the drinks?" Jessie said.

"I spoke to the maid when I arrived. It's just her and her mother who cooks on the staff. They come in from Chipping Norton when the house is in use by the Oxford College that owns it, apparently," Flo answered. "Maybe she's helping as they are short in numbers."

They were halfway to the stones now, and the path turned sharply left in order to wind its way up the steepening rise of the hill. The wind whipped across them with an iciness Flo could feel sinking to her bones. They made the rest of the quick trip in silence.

The stones themselves were a moss-covered and gnarled group, the wind and rain over the centuries having battered and bruised them until they had taken their current pockmarked form. Each one coming up to around Flo's waist in height, the circle ran some one hundred feet in diameter and the group naturally formed a smaller circle within the stone one, with the solicitor Hove at the centre. He smiled at the others as Stammerthwaite handed out steaming mugs of hot cider.

Once everyone had a cup, Hove reached into the inside pocket of his coat and produced an envelope, which he tore open methodically before pulling a single sheet of paper from it.

"My instructions are to read this letter to all guests at this very spot, then we can return to the house and warm up," he said in a light, good-humoured manner. He held the paper in front of him and read. "You are gathered here, in this place, in order to hear the last will and testament of Mr Gordon Montague Badala. This reading will take place in two stages, of which this is the first. The second will take place on the third day you spend at Standings, on the day you leave. On that third day, the full amount of the estate will be revealed and divided amongst the remaining parties."

"Remaining parties?" Henry said from Flo's side.

Hove gave him a stern look.

"Please, do not interrupt again, Mr Bitten," the lawyer said before clearing his throat and continuing. "Now we come to the first part of the statement. There are two stipulations to receiving your share of the inheritance. One, as has already been stated, you must stay at Standings for two nights until you are told you can leave by myself, at the conclusion of events. Anyone who leaves the estate before that time forfeits their right to any share of the fortune, and the remaining guests' share will increase. The second stipulation..."

There was a pause as the lawyer seemed to grip the paper in his hand more tightly, pulling it closer to his face as his eyes, widening, darted back and forth across the text in front of him.

The wind whipped around the stones, fluttering the coattails of those gathered as the silence spread into an unease.

"For goodness' sake, man," Edward Buckley exclaimed, "can you get on with the proceedings before we all freeze to death?"

Hove looked up at his words, and for a moment his mouth opened and shut like a fish thrown onto land. He took a deep breath, nodded, and his eyes returned to the paper.

"The second stipulation," he began, his voice sounding different now, his previous fine china accent breaking slightly with hints of Cockney, "is that before the end of your stay at Standings, the true circumstance of the death of Elina Fortesque must be determined."

It felt to Flo as if time had suddenly frozen. The gusting wind had stilled, the steam from the cup she held in her hand frozen in the air as her entire body tensed. A loud crash from behind her broke the moment. She turned to see Juliet Atoll's maid, her eyes wide in horror, but not at the mess of mud, wine and glass at her feet, nor the silver tray which rolled in a circle around them. Her eyes were on the lawyer, Hove.

Flo looked at Jessie and saw her grey eyes wide as she scanned the gathered circle. She felt a hand in hers and turned to see George looking at her with concern.

"What on earth can it mean?" he said, his voice desperate.

"I, I don't know," Flo answered, her voice thick with emotion.

T he party had arrived back at the house in a more muddled, less orderly manner than they had left.

The Buckleys headed up the stairs to their room without a word to anyone. Juliet Atoll admonished her maid in harsh, but whispered tones in the drawing's corner room as George, Henry, Jessie and Flo mixed drinks from the cabinet and huddled in the opposite corner.

"What the bloody hell is all this about?" Henry said in an angry hiss. "Is it someone's idea of a joke? Because it isn't funny in the slightest."

"Are you OK?" George said to Flo, who was staring at her drink with wide eyes.

"I just don't understand," she answered with a shake of her head.

"Elina Fortesque," Jessie said softly, a British tone to her accent once more rising to the fore. "Was she your friend that passed away?"

Flo nodded.

"But what on earth has this Badala got to do with it?" Henry said.

"How did she die?" Jessie asked.

Her three companions' eyes darted between each other for a moment before Flo answered.

"She was murdered while walking home one night. They never found her killer."

"I see," Jessie said, her eyes widening. "Well, now at least it's clear why we're all here."

"Is it?" George asked.

"Damned if I can see," Henry added.

"This Mr Badala, whoever he is, has gathered this little audience as he believes one of the group knows who murdered your friend, or even did the deed themselves."

George gave a gasp, turning to her in horror.

"What an awful thing to say. Tell me you don't mean that!"

"Can you think of another reason for these

AG BARNETT

circumstances? Badala is offering a reward, of sorts, for the conclusion of a murder case."

"But what has this Badala chap got to do with what happened to Elina?" George asked.

"An excellent question," Flo said, looking across to where Juliet Atoll was still admonishing her maid. "Another is why exactly this guest list was put together."

"Well," George said, "it's pretty obvious that the three of us would be invited as guests. The four of us used to knock about together a fair deal. So the three of us being here makes some sense, I suppose."

"That doesn't mean we had anything to do with her death," Flo said in an angered tone.

"No," Jessie said thoughtfully, "But it might mean this Badala chap hasn't got a clue who did and is just gathering people who were connected to Elina somehow."

"But I've never seen any of these people," Flo said, "and I don't remember Elina mentioning any of them."

Jessie's eyes drifted over her shoulder as the solicitor, Jonathon Hove, entered the room.

"Well," she said, nodding towards him, "here's the person most likely to be able to tell us."

Hove's eyes darted around the room before landing on the sideboard behind them where the drinks lay, and he made a beeline for it. He gave them a brief smile before making himself a large whiskey and soda.

"So, Mr Hove," Jessie said when he turned back to the room. "That was all very melodramatic."

He gave a nervous chuckle from the back of his throat. "It was rather."

"It seemed to take you by surprise as well?" Flo continued.

His head jerked up to look at her suddenly before his eyes scanned the small group.

"I didn't know what was going to be in the announcement, no."

"Seems a bit unusual for the legal chap handling the estate?" Henry asked.

"If you'll excuse me, I have to contact my office," Hove said hurriedly, and headed for the exit.

"Well, that wasn't suspicious at all," Flo muttered as she watched him leave.

"Well," Edward said as his wife closed the door to their room behind her, "you wanted to know why we're here. Now we do."

Anna's face was pale, her eyes darting about the room as she began pacing.

"I need to think," she said.

"Perhaps we should leave?" Edward offered as he slumped into one of the two wing-backed armchairs.

"No!" Anna said sharply. "I don't know what Badala's game is, but I see no reason for us to not receive part of his estate as he intended."

"But this damned Fortesque woman!" Edward said, banging his fist on the dressing table.

"You mustn't get excited, Edward, nothing good will come of that." She continued to pace up and down the room. "What we need now are cool heads. No one here can connect us with that woman unless we let ourselves down." She stopped pacing and turned to him. "By that, I mean not letting the situation get the better of us and allow ourselves to panic."

"Yes, yes, quite right, of course," he answered gruffly.

"Good," she said with a nod of her head, before the pacing continued. "As I see it, we have two days to get through before we receive our share of the estate. Although remaining here might be part of the legal agreement, I'm sure they won't be able to enforce this nonsense about finding out who murdered the wretched girl. So we sit tight, keep ourselves to ourselves and then claim our legacy at the end of the two days."

"It's all dashed odd," Edward grumbled.

"We must make the best of the situation," Anna said decisively, but continued her pacing. Suggesting to her husband that she wasn't as sure as she sounded.

CHAPTER

FOURTEEN

"Just exactly what is all this?" Jonathon Hove asked in a hiss as he entered the dining room where Stammerthwaite was laying the table for dinner.

"Sir?" he said, rising and turning to him slowly.

"You know exactly what I mean," Jonathan said, moving towards him. "What on earth has all this got to do with Elina Fortesque?"

"Did you know Miss Fortesque, sir?" the butler said in a tone of mild surprise, his left eyebrow rising above his eye patch.

The common but strange presentation of this facial expression threw Jonathan for a moment. This man really was one of the most extraordinary chaps he'd ever seen. That large, domed head which seemed to have risen through his long, lank grey hair like an egg appearing from an unkempt chicken. That thick, grey beard which surrounded the thin mouth, all set against skin like leather. He would have made a fantastic pirate on the stage.

"No," Jonathan said eventually, "I didn't know any Miss Fortesque. But what is all this stuff about her being murdered? Are you telling me that one of the people here killed her?"

"I'm sorry, sir. As I informed you before, Mr Badala merely hired me to perform my duties and to hand you the documents I did earlier."

"And you still maintain you don't know who this Badala is or why he wanted all these people here?"

"I'm sorry I can't put your mind at rest, sir," the man said solemnly. "As I explained before, I was hired through an agency and never had the pleasure of meeting Mr Badala personally."

"This whole thing stinks to high heaven." Jonathan Hove shook his head ruefully. "There are other papers coming. Where are they?"

"I assume they will be delivered to the house when they are needed, sir. I don't have them yet, I'm afraid."

"Oh!" a voice cried from behind Jonathan. He turned to see a mousey young girl with thick-rimmed spectacles that magnified her eyes to the size of dinner plates. He recognised her as the maid of one of the guests.

"I'm sorry," she said, giving a small curtsy, "I thought it was just Mr Stammerthwaite in here." Her eyes moved to the dining table behind them and widened.

"I think you've miscounted the places for dinner, Mr Stammerthwaite."

"As I have told you, Miss Fielding, there were eight in the invited party, and one unexpected guest," Stammerthwaite said flatly.

"Please, Mr Stammerthwaite!" she said, her voice rising in pitch as she pleaded. "It's not right!"

Jonathan decided to leave them arguing the point. It appeared he would get no answers here.

CHAPTER

FIFTEEN

J uliet had watched her maid scurry out of the room a few minutes ago. Since then, she had been gazing at the closed door with her head bowed, trying to shallow her breathing.

She knew that the group across the room was watching her. Had they heard her conversation? No, she decided. She and Kate had been talking in hushed tones and the group was too far away.

To say it rattled her would be an understatement. One should never expect your own staff to believe you are capable of murder. Then again, was she really so entirely innocent? It worried her she wasn't sure herself.

She took a deep breath and moved across to

the group with her head held high. She needed to keep up appearances now more than ever.

"I see you have all done the sensible thing and got yourself a drink," she said as she reached them.

"Can I get you one?" George asked.

"I'd be ever so grateful," she replied. "Staff can be so trying."

"She looked pretty upset," Flo said, glancing towards the door the maid had left through.

"Oh, don't worry about her, silly girl loses her head over the slightest thing."

"The slightest thing in this case being at an event designed to uncover a murderer?" Jessie said with a mischievous smile.

"I'm afraid I can't remember any of your names," Juliet continued, ignoring the comment. "Always been terrible at them."

George returned to the group with her drink and gave the introductions.

A moment of awkward silence followed before the door to the drawing room opened again and the Buckleys came through it, followed by the solicitor Hove, providing a welcome distraction.

"If you'd like to help yourself to drinks," Hove said, directing them towards the sideboard before clapping his hands together and rubbing them as he spoke.

"Now, I'm sure you all have a lot of questions, but I'm afraid I don't have any answers." The group, which had turned to face him as one as he began, looked on in silence.

"I was as unaware of the contents of that letter as you were. They instructed me to open it only at that moment."

"Do you have any other instructions you haven't opened?" Henry asked from Flo's side.

There was the slightest pause before Hove replied.

"No, there is only one other document to be opened this weekend, and that is at the conclusion."

"Well, open the damned thing now!" Edward Buckley rumbled.

"I don't have it yet. It's being sent here, by hand, on Sunday."

Hove made his own way to the drinks cabinet and poured himself a large glass of whiskey from the decanter as the rest of the group watched him in an uneasy silence.

"You must know something about all this?" Edward continued. "What sort of law firm are you if you're going around dragging people into the middle of nowhere and then accusing them of murder?"

"No one accused anyone of murder," his wife said irritably.

"As good as damn well did," Edward grumbled as his moustache vanished into his whiskey tumbler again.

"I take it you all knew Elina Fortesque?" Jessie said.

"We've never even heard the name before," Anna Buckley said quickly, causing her husband to glance at her before looking around at the group.

"George, Henry and I were friends with her," Flo said, her voice a little shaky.

"The name means nothing to me, I'm afraid," Juliet Atoll said in a calm tone.

"If you were friends of this person," Edward Buckley said, staring at Flo, "then it seems to me that you'd be the best people to shed light on this business?"

Flo looked around the group, feeling the intensity of so many suspicious eyes cast towards her. She swallowed, trying to find the courage to answer, when Henry stepped in and spoke.

"As Flo says, Elina was our friend. Six months

ago, she was murdered in a small park in London on her way home."

Silence rolled across the room, with only the crackling of the fire in the grate to show that time hadn't simply frozen.

"How was she murdered?" Jessie asked, causing Flo to jump at the sudden break in the tension.

Henry cleared his throat before answering. "They hit her across the head."

"Really!" Edward Buckley said. "Must we talk of such things with ladies present?!"

"I rather think that's the point of you all being assembled here," Jessie answered, a slightly sly smile on her face. "This Mr Badala has gathered you here for a reason. Apparently, that reason is to discover the circumstances around Elina Fortesque's death." She turned to Flo. "I assume they have found no one responsible for her murder?" Flo shook her head.

Jessie took a long sip of her drink as her eyes moved slowly across every face in the room, clearly aware that she had their full attention and was enjoying it.

"I rather think that the dear departed Mr Badala believes that one of you is responsible. As

Mr Buckley says, you are all being accused of murder. I think the question we all need to think very carefully about is... is he right?"

Now the eyes of the group left her and instead darted across the gathered faces. Flo watched them sizing each other up, scrutinising every blink, every twitch of the mouth. All of them, looking for signs of a killer.

She shuddered and clutched her glass close to her chest as tears formed in her eyes.

After the dramatic events of the afternoon, the guests had gradually all given their excuses before retiring to their rooms to brood on their situation until the dinner gong had rung.

Seated at a long table with liberal bottles of wine, it appeared to Flo as though everyone was making a concerted effort to talk of anything but Elina Fortesque and their reason for being called to Standings House.

In particular, what satisfied everyone's desire for a distraction was the empty place setting once everyone was seated.

"Bloody staff can't count," chuckled Henry.

"Maybe it's been set for someone who died

here," Jessie said enthusiastically, "like a mark of respect."

"Stammerthwaite," Edward Buckley hollered as the man followed a young maid in who was carrying a large silver bowl of soup. "Why is there an empty place setting?"

"I'm afraid, sir," Stammerthwaite said in his slow, dry voice, "that one of the guests has declined to be seated."

"Declined to be seated?" Henry said, looking around the table.

Gradually, the sound of cutlery on china fell silent, as all eyes turned to the butler. His one eye was turned towards the wall across the table, where Juliet Atoll's maid was standing, flat against the wall as though clinging on for dear life. She let out a sharp cry before dashing to Juliet's side.

"I'm so sorry, miss, I told him I didn't want to!"

"What on earth are you talking about?" Juliet said, her eyes wide, cheeks reddening.

"Miss Fielding is in fact, a guest of Mr Badala's," Stammerthwaite boomed.

There was a sharp intake of breath from Anna Buckley, and a dazed silence from the rest of the group.

Juliet Atoll was staring at her maid as though

she had just grown a new head.

"What is this man talking about, Kate?" she demanded.

"I...I... It's not my fault, miss!" The girl squealed, reaching into her dress pocket and pulling out a well-worn envelope and fumbling it open.

Juliet took the letter that was held out to her and her eyes scanned it, widening as she did so.

"This must be some kind of joke?!" she retorted.

"When it came, I couldn't believe my luck," the unfortunate Kate mumbled, a tear rolling down her cheek. "I was going to ask for a couple of days off to come down and see what it was all about. I started dreaming about what I could do with a nice bit of money." She paused, and looked up, suddenly aware that the eyes of the entire room were on her. "And then you opened your letter and said we were coming right to this place and I couldn't believe it! I didn't know what to do and then..." She looked up at her employer with a look of such pure fear that it even softened Juliet's sharp features for a moment.

"Kate?" she whispered, but the young woman merely sobbed and ran from the room.

E dward was drinking too much. Although Anna had seen this pattern play out a thousand times, this time, there could be consequences. She leaned towards her husband's ear.

"Just because there are ample bottles of wine on the table," she whispered to him, "it does not mean they expect you to drink them all."

He turned to her with glassy eyes and a reddening nose.

"Don't worry, darling," he hissed back. "We don't have to pay for the bloody stuff!"

He maintained eye contact with her as he purposefully filled his glass again with red wine, spilling some on the white tablecloth as he did so.

Anna turned away, unable to look at him any more, and saw one of the table's occupants staring at Edward. It was the floppy-haired young man with the thick glasses and a rather simple expression.

He noticed her then and gave a sympathetic smile before turning away. She couldn't bear that people were seeing what a spectacle Edward was making of himself. In fact, she was actually rather thankful that the frightful fuss with the maid had happened. Surely that would be what stuck in people's minds after this ghastly dinner.

"You know," Edward said in a breathy whisper in her ear, "I think I know that chap from somewhere."

"Of course you do, dear," she replied automatically, before turning to smile at the solicitor Hove. There was something about his manner that she recognised in herself.

She had been the only daughter of a grocer, her mother having died in childbirth. She had married Edward when his shipping company was only in its infancy, but she could see the potential. More in the company than in her husband.

As the company had expanded and become more successful, she had grown to love the finer things in life. She often thought she had been born into the wrong family. She had the soul of a wealthy heiress coming from old money. Not the daughter of a grubby grocer who had to back the right horse, metaphorically speaking, to achieve her status.

Unfortunately, Edward had not turned out to be a thoroughbred. He was a simple man, without a head for business like his partner. His uncompli-cated ways betrayed an uncomplicated mind. Any career progress he had made had come through 'looking the right sort,' and thick-headed bluster. Of course, being lucky enough to find a partner who actually knew what he was doing had helped. She shuddered slightly and her thoughts returned to the man in front of her. Yes, he was playing a part—so who was the real Hove, she wondered?

"What on earth are you doing here?" Henry said quietly to Juliet Atoll, who sat on his right.

"I received an invitation, as I assume, you did," she replied, her eyes scanning the diners who were engaged in conversation with others next to them.

Henry stole a glance at her as he took a sip of his wine. It felt like years since he had seen her, but it had only been a matter of weeks. She had been cold on that occasion, as she seemed to be now. Though that could purely be down to the awkward situation they now found themselves in.

No one must know they knew each other. They had to be careful.

Until the time of Elina's death, their clandestine meetings had always been explosive, passionate affairs. Just like they had been since they were old enough to understand such feelings.

Elina's death. Had Juliet simply been using him? No, she loved him still. He knew it deep in his bones. He just needed to talk to her properly, away from this gaggle of odd characters and this gloomy house. Then there was the money. An inheritance like this could solve all their problems. They could put this ghastly charade behind them and finally be together, but if that relied on revealing the circumstances surrounding Elina's death...

"Are you OK?" George said to Flo, who was on his right.

"Yes, thank you," she replied with a small smile.

"Um...,"...he replied.

Funny how something as simple as a smile can make a chap all tongue-tied. She was so delicate, so vulnerable. Like a fine china doll.

"A bit troubling all this," he stammered, "upsetting, not fair to you. Understand if you'd want to leave."

Flo set her knife and fork down and placed one hand on his. "It's sweet of you to worry about me," she said with another smile that made his stomach somersault, "but I can't leave now.

Whoever arranged this clearly believes someone here knows something about Elina's death. If that's the case, I have to stay."

"Of course, of course. Well, I'll be here with you."

"Thank you," she said, squeezing his hand before letting go and picking up the conversation with Jessie across the table from them.

The American had been staring down the table at something before her lively face turned back with a wide smile.

She was an odd character, that was for sure. Far too brazen and bold for his liking, and this seemed to be highlighted even more when next to Flo and her soft way.

It was strange, her latching on to them like this. He would have to monitor her. He had to protect Flo.

CHAPTER

TWENTY

T here had only been the briefest of post-dinner drinks before the new residents of Standings House made their way to their rooms. After what had felt like one of the longest days of her life, Flo had climbed into the vaguely musty bed and been asleep within seconds.

It was from that same bed that she now woke with a start.

She sat up quickly from under the heavy bedcovers, her eyes straining in the almost pitch-black room. The only light in the room came from the dying embers of the fire, the heat of which had now almost entirely gone from the room.

The sound that had woken her pierced the

darkness again. A squeaking and grinding of metal. Her heart, already thumping in her chest, threatened to burst clear through her rib cage. The sound was the doorknob of her room turning.

Before she could even process the information, there was a change in pressure in the room and she knew the door was opening. She scrambled on to her feet, standing on the mattress of the bed tensed, ready to run.

"Flo?" a whispered voice came from the doorway as a lit candle swung into view, blinding her. "What on earth are you doing stood on the bed?"

Flo sagged as she recognised the American tones of Jessie Circle. The candlelight bobbed forwards, and she heard the door close.

"You scared me half to death!" Flo hissed at her as the candle moved in the darkness to the side of the bed.

"I knocked" Jessie shrugged, holding the candle to her face so her excited features were illuminated in a ghostly fashion. "But I had to do it quietly, so I didn't alert our nighttime prowler."

"Prowler?" Flo asked, her hand moving to her chest as a prickle of fear ran up her neck.

"Yes! Why do you think I'm calling on you in

the dead of night? It's not to see what taste in nightgowns you have." Her eyes scanned down Flo's plain white nightgown that hung shapelessly off her thin frame. "Although I must say, you could definitely find something more flattering."

Flo clambered down off the bed so she was face-to-face with her.

"What do you mean 'prowler'?"

"I heard someone moving about outside my room, in the corridor, so I lit a candle and went to investigate."

"What on earth did you do that for? It's probably just someone going to get a glass of water!"

"As I opened my door, I swear I heard footsteps running away, so I hurried out, but there was no one there."

"I'm sure it was just your imagination playing tricks on you."

Jessie raised one eyebrow in a look made only more withering by the flickering flame between them.

"I am not easily tricked, Flo," she said flatly before a mischievous smile returned. "Even by my imagination. Come on, let's see who's up to what, shall we?"

Flo sighed in resignation as Jessie took her

arm, leading her towards the door. "It's pitch black out there," she said as Jessie opened the door with the same creak of metal and peered out into the gloom.

"The power's out," Jessie answered in a whisper. "Must be the storm."

They stepped out into the hallway, their candlelight casting only a weak pale of light in either direction. As soon as they had stepped out of the door, they heard raised voices. Muffled and distant, but full of a vicious, snapping anger.

"It's coming from this way," Jessie said as she pulled her down the corridor, which ran away from Flo's room along the front of the house. A gust of air rushed towards them, causing the candle to flicker out as the thud of a door slamming came from somewhere ahead.

They froze in the dark, Flo clinging onto Jessie's arm.

More doors seem to bang in the distance as floorboards creaked from footsteps unseen.

"Come on," Jessie said, pulling Flo forward into the gloom.

They walked on slowly as their eyes adjusted to the darkness enough to at least make out the walls. They reached the corner as the door in front of them opened, blinding them with the sudden rectangle of light from the room.

"What's going on?" Juliet said as she peered out at them.

"We were wondering the same thing," Jessie said, squinting as she shielded her eyes with her hands.

"Is everyone all right?" a voice came from their right, making them all jump. George stepped into the light from the door in blue and white pyjamas and holding a fire poker in one hand.

"Goodness, George," Flo laughed at the sight of him, "were you planning on tackling an intruder with that?!"

He reddened and looked at the poker somewhat sheepishly. "Well, you know. Noises in the dark and all that."

"I saw him come out with the thing," Henry said, coming up behind him with a chuckle. "Looked like quite the fierce character." He punched him on the shoulder playfully, turning George's slightly puzzled face an even deeper shade of red.

"Did any of you hear someone arguing?" Flo asked.

"Arguing?" Juliet said. "At this time of night?"

"It must have been the Buckleys," Henry said. "Only married people argue in the dead of the night."

"Well, whoever it was, they seem to have stopped now," George said. "I'm going back to bed."

Murmured agreements from the others spilled out before they all headed back to their rooms.

"Good night again, Jessie," Flo said as she reached their two rooms, which stood next to each other. "I trust I can count on you not waking me again before breakfast?"

"Maybe." Jessie shrugged, her eyes looking over Flo's shoulder at Henry. Once his bedroom door had clicked shut, she leaned forward and spoke in a conspiratorial whisper.

"Listen Flo, I'm a suspicious character and I can smell when something doesn't feel right. Something isn't right here. I want you to go in and lock your door now, and don't open it to anyone unless you hear me with them as well."

She pushed Flo into her room and closed the door before she could respond.

Flo swayed lightly in a shocked daze before moving forward and locking the door.

CHAPTER

TWENTY-ONE

J uliet leaned back against her bedroom door, breathing hard.

"No one knows, no one knows," she whispered to herself repeatedly in the flickering light from the single candle to her side.

How many times had she said those words? They had become a mantra to her. To be repeated in those dark, frightening times when she was sure her secret was out. When she was sure she would be caught, exposed, and her entire life would come crumbling down around her.

Now, though, those words seemed to bring no comfort at all. The pounding of her heart in her chest did not recede, nor did the light, dizzy feeling of panic in her head.

Her secret wasn't even the thing that worried her the most. What worried her most was that her suspicions had been right.

CHAPTER
TWENTY-TWO

W hy lie? Why would Henry have done that?

That's what raced through George's mind as he lay in his bed, sheets pulled tight around him in the pitch-black darkness.

People didn't lie for no good reason, only to hide something.

He turned on his side with a worried frown. He had to make sure Flo was safe. Whatever was happening here in this blasted cold and draughty house, he needed to protect Flo.

CHAPTER

TWENTY-THREE

He was sleeping now, thank god.

Anna Buckley watched the slow rise and fall of her husband's chest, his mouth slack and open as whistled and grunted in their bed.

She finished her glass of whiskey and stood up with a sigh. It was time to deal with him.

TWENTY-FOUR

W hy had he lied? Not that it mattered. Nothing mattered now.

Henry knew he should never have put this whole stupid plan in motion. It had caused nothing but stress and worry. Turning them both into paranoid shadows of themselves, eyeing each other with suspicion.

They were in too deep and had gone too far to back down now, though. They had to see this through. It would be worth it in the end.

He sighed as he ran through the all too brief conversation they'd had. None of it made any sense.

TWENTY-FIVE

Flo listened to the wind and rain hammering at the thin panes of her bedroom window as she tried to brush her wiry blonde hair into some sort of resemblance of respectability.

She had just managed to at least semi-flatten the sizeable chunk of her hair that had pointed directly at the ceiling that morning when the knock came on her bedroom door. She gave up on the hopeless task and went to answer.

"Goodness," Jessie said as the door swung open, "did you sleep with your head hanging out the window last night?"

"I know, it's a disaster," Flo answered with a

sigh as she moved aside to let Jessie in. "I'm just going to clip it back."

"How do you think everyone slept after our excitement in the night?" Jessie asked as she moved to the window.

"Hopefully better than me," Flo said as she swept her hair to one side and added grips. "The wind and rain battered my window so hard at one point I thought it was going to break."

"It was quite the storm," Jessie agreed as she peered out into the dull morning. "The river looks like it might burst its banks."

"Really?" Flo said, rushing to the window.

Jessie had not been exaggerating. The river which ran along the base of the deep valley was a foaming, frothing torrent that rushed under the bridge that led to the house at an alarming rate.

"My goodness," she breathed, in awe at the raw power of the river.

"Oh, don't worry, I'm sure it will ease off today," Jessie answered breezily. "Shall we head down?"

Flo gave one last look at the thick, dark grey clouds stacked high in the sky and didn't feel Jessie's confidence. She turned and smiled, taking the arm that Jessie held out to her before heading out of her room.

They saw no one in the house until they reached the dining room, where breakfast lay on a long side table against one wall. Anna Buckley sat on the other side of the dining table, which had been laid with a crisp white tablecloth. The smell of bacon and toast caused Flo a sharp pang of hunger, and she pulled free of Jessie's arm and headed for the array of food.

"Good morning, Mrs Buckley," Jessie said brightly as Flo moved away. "Is Mr Buckley less of an early riser than you?"

"I'm afraid Mr Buckley is unwell," Anna answered quickly. "He will remain in our rooms today."

"I'm sorry to hear that," Flo said, adding a strip of crisp bacon to her plate. "I hope he can take some food in his room?"

"Later, perhaps," Anna said.

"Morning all," George said as he came through the door, followed by Juliet and Henry. "I'm famished."

"Well, you're in luck," Jessie said, gesturing at the spread. "This may be a strange situation, but at least they seem to feed us well."

"Just like they do with pigs who are going to be slaughtered," Henry said.

"Someone's woken up in a maudlin mood," Flo said.

"Funny how certain company will do that," he muttered in response, but when Flo looked up at him, he was busying himself, loading his plate with food.

"Did everyone manage to sleep through the storm last night?" Jessie said as she took a seat at the table with Flo.

"Last night? It's still going, isn't it?" Juliet said as she sat down opposite them. Flo noted she had added a solitary piece of toast to her plate, which she had buttered only lightly before beginning to cut it into delicate triangles.

"True," Jessie replied, "I was saying to Flo that the river looks like it might well burst its banks."

"I hope not," Henry said. "That would mean we're all stuck here."

"Aren't we all stuck here, anyway?" Juliet Atoll said in a sharp tone. "If we want the money, that is?"

Henry dropped his half-full plate down onto the table with a clatter before leaning forward, balled fists on the dining table as he stared across at her.

"I think what you mean to say," he said, his jaw clenched tight, "is that we're all here until we uncover a murderer."

There was a deathly silence around the room as all eyes turned to him. Forks wavered halfway to mouths, bacon sat half cut.

"One of us here," he continued, his voice steadier now, but no less angry, "stalked Elina in that park and killed her in cold blood." He turned to Juliet Atoll, who was looking at him with her eyes like saucers against her pale skin. "And it wasn't me!" At the last word, he slammed his hand down on the table in front of them, causing everyone to jump in their seats.

"Now, steady on, old chap," George said, but Henry was already stalking towards the door. As he disappeared through it, the striking figure of the butler, Stammerthwaite, appeared.

"Excuse me for interrupting your breakfast," he gave a small nod of his head, "but I was wondering if any of you had seen Mr Hove this morning?"

There was a general murmur of negative

responses, the party still dazed from Henry's outburst.

"I'm afraid he isn't answering his door, and it appears to be locked."

There was a clang of cutlery on porcelain as Jessie jumped up from her seat.

"Do you have another key for the door?" she said in an urgent voice.

"No, miss," the butler replied with a frown. "All the bedrooms have one key for its occupants' use."

Jessie gave a brief nod and then looked at Flo.

"Could you come with me for a moment?"

"Of course," Flo answered, slightly bemused as she followed the American from the room, giving a shrug to a questioning look from George as she did so.

"What exactly are we going to do?" Flo asked as they moved up the wide staircase.

"I want to check if our Mr Hove is in his room or not."

"But if he won't answer?"

They had reached the wide landing now and turned to their left towards Hove's door. Jessie paused before it, and fixed Flo with a penetrating stare.

"I'd prefer it if you kept what I'm about to do to yourself for the time being."

Flo felt her pulse quicken.

"Of course," she answered with a nervous laugh. Jessie stared at her a moment longer and then reached into her trouser pocket and brought out a long, thin wrap of black cloth which she unwound quickly. Inside, stored in individually sewn pockets within, were sheathed a row of four metal utensils that Flo couldn't identify. She selected one and bent to the lock of the door, sliding it in gently.

Flo looked over her shoulder as a thrill of adrenaline ran down her spine.

"Are you picking the lock?!" she said in a hushed whisper.

There was a soft click.

"Yes," Jessie said, straightening, "not that it needed much picking. It's a simple enough affair. Ready?"

Her hand moved to the doorknob, and Flo took in a deep breath before nodding.

"Ready."

Jessie opened the door, and they both peered in. It was empty.

Flo frowned as she followed Jessie into the room. It was a simple enough space, similar to her room. A bed, side tables, an extensive wardrobe. Jessie moved to the corner of the room and opened the door, which led to the small bathroom. She turned back, shaking her head.

"If he's not in here," Flo said, "then Mrs Buckley was right, he must have just gone for a walk."

"Why would he lock his door?" Jessie asked.

"Maybe he has something of value here. We are all strangers after all, no reason one of us couldn't be a burglar of some kind." She gave a small gasp and looked up at Jessie, feeling her face reddening. "I didn't mean to suggest that you... I mean, you do have a set of lock picks, but that doesn't mean."

Jessie broke into a broad grin. "Oh, don't be silly, of course I'm..." A shout from the window interrupted her. They both turned to it and Flo realised with surprise that it was wide open.

They rushed towards it, sticking their heads out into the driving rain.

Below them, kneeling in the sodden grass, dark hair plastered across his forehead, was Henry

Bitten. As though sensing their gazes on him from above, he looked up, his eyes wide and wild. In front of him lay the crumpled body of Jonathan Hove.

"Touch nothing!" Jessie called down to Henry, who blinked rain from his eyes before giving a quick nod.

"Come on," Jessie said, "we have to get down there and see if there are any clues the rain hasn't washed away."

"Clues?" Flo said, her voice cracking as the room seemed to swim around her.

"You don't think he died accidentally, do you?" Jessie said as she took her arm and began leading her to the door. "Our Mr Hove, if that was his name, has been murdered."

Flo tried to respond, but found that the air seemed to have been sucked from her lungs. She focused on not falling as they descended the stairs.

How could Hove have been murdered? Her mind was racing with the various possibilities. The most startling of which was the thought that if Hove had been murdered, it must have been someone at the house. The isolated position of the house, and the fierce weather, seemed to rule out the possibility of an outsider having committed the act.

As they threw their coats over the shoulders, she looked at Jessie's face, which was alive with excitement. Grey eyes gleaming, her full mouth closed in a half smile. Flo realised with a pang of shock that her new American friend was enjoying this. As they stepped out into the driving rain, Flo's mind returned to the lock picks Jessie had had. How much did she really know about her?

"My god, it's wild out here!" Jessie shouted back at her over the blustering wind.

They made their way to the right around the corner of the house and hurried to Henry, who was now leaning back against the wall of the house, staring out into the torrential rain.

"Are you OK?" Flo asked him, firmly trying to keep her eyes from the prone figure in the grass.

"Of course I'm not bloody OK!" he snapped,

before his face instantly softened. "I'm sorry, Flo, it's just..."

"It's all right," she said, lifting her coat higher so that he could duck his head under it as well.

"His neck is broken," Jessie said.

Flo turned to see her stooped over Hove's body and felt her stomach tighten. Jessie rose and began stalking the area around.

"What's she doing?" Henry said.

"Looking for clues, apparently."

"What is she? Some kind of female Sherlock Holmes?"

Flo frowned. "Actually, I'm worried she might be more of a Moriarty."

"What?"

"Oh, nothing," she said as Jessie hurried back to them.

"There's nothing around here. We need to get him back inside. Flo, you and I can take a leg each, Henry. You get the head end."

"You can't be serious?!" Henry said, a note of horror in his voice.

"No," Flo said, almost unable to believe the words were leaving her lips, "Jessie's right. We can't leave him out here. We need to take him into the house."

Henry's dark eyes flicked between them and, realising they were serious, or possibly just right, he swore under his breath and moved towards Hove's body.

CHAPTER

TWENTY-SEVEN

The final journey back to the house for Jonathan Hove had not been a dignified one, and Henry couldn't help but feel that he was responsible. His hands shook as he struck a match to light a cigarette. He felt as though he could still hear the soft thud of Hove's slack head hitting the turf when Henry had slipped on the wet earth.

"I guess this rules out a game of billiards for the rest of the weekend," he said, trying to make light of the situation. It didn't sound convincing, even to his own ears.

In front of him, laid out across the green baize of the table, Jonathan Hove lay. The man who had apparently gathered them all here in the first place on behalf of his client, Mr Badala.

The fearful-looking butler had crabbed his way off to phone for the police, so he supposed there was nothing to do other than to get out of his wet clothes.

"I'm going to get changed," he said to Flo and Jessie, who were both staring at the body as though hypnotised. Flo was pale, her mouth pinched. In shock, or so it looked at him.

This American, though, she looked positively aglow with the situation. The red blush on her cheeks seemed to speak more to excitement than horror. As if to confirm his thoughts, she darted forward and began looking through the pockets of the deceased lawyer.

"I thought you said not to touch anything?" he protested.

"That instruction was for you," she answered distractedly. "Not for me."

She pulled a battered leather wallet from Hove's jacket pocket and rifled through it. She took out a small square of paper and unfolded it.

"It's a newspaper cutting," she said as she opened it out fully.

Henry moved round the billiard table to look

over her shoulder, Flo doing the same on the other side.

"The cast of Fulham theatre's production of *The Babes in the Woods*," Jessie read aloud from the tagline above the photo.

"Look!" Flo said with a squawk, her finger pointing to the figure on the right-hand side of the group.

Henry recognised the long, thin face immediately. It was the lawyer that lay dead before them, Mr Jonathan Hove. His eyes ran along the list of names which ran under the photo until he reached the corresponding one.

"Frank Sparkes," he said aloud.

"Either our lawyer moonlights as an actor," Flo said slowly, "or we have an actor pretending to be a lawyer."

TWENTY-EIGHT

J uliet had to cling on to the bottom post of
the stairs in fear of falling over.

"What do you mean, dead?" she said in
a hoarse whisper.

"What do you think I mean?!" Henry snapped
back, his rage apparently not dissipated from the
breakfast table.

"But how?" she stammered.

"Murdered, according to Miss Circle in there."
He jerked his thumb back towards the billiard
room where she had seen him exit as she had
reached the stairs, heading back to her room.

"Why are you soaking wet?" she exclaimed,
only now realising water was dripping from him
onto the floor.

His lips pursed, and she noticed his hands clenched into fists.

"I was angry," he answered through gritted teeth. "I went outside to cool off and found Hove dead on the grass."

He glared at her for a moment.

"Was he...," Juliet began quietly, "dead when you found him?"

"I knew it!" He roared at her, rearing up, his face flushing red. "You think I killed her, don't you?"

Despite his ferocity, she felt aware of movement in the hallway and turned to see Anna Buckley and George Wilson coming out of the dining room, no doubt to see what the noise was about. Almost simultaneously, Flo Hammond and Jessie Circle emerged from the billiard room.

She turned back to him, opening her mouth to stop him, to give some sign that others were there, that they could talk about this later. Instead, she gaped like the fish her fiancé, Lord Perciville Baxter, landed with glee each weekend.

"That's it, isn't it?" he said, looking at her with a mix of fury and disgust now. "Or maybe it was you who killed her, and I'm just the convenient chump who you've marked to hang for it?"

"Steady on, Henry," George Wilson said, approaching them.

Henry whipped round, finally noticing their audience. Juliet saw his shoulders sag slightly, the clenched fists at his side loosen.

"I'm going to dry off," he said in a low voice before turning back towards the stairs. He gave Juliet a hard, brutal glare as he passed her, stomping up the stairs.

"Are you OK?"

Juliet tore her gaze from his receding figure to turn to the speaker. It was Miss Hammond, looking up at her with blue eyes wide, her short blonde bob pulled close to her head.

"I'm fine, thank you," Juliet answered, raising her chin.

The others were gathering round now, as though waiting for some sort of explanation for the scene they had just witnessed.

"I believe Mr Bitten is just rather overwrought at having discovered Mr Hove's body."

This drew gasps from George Wilson and Anna Buckley, who had clearly been unaware of the news. The group immediately exploded into questions and answers, and she knew she had done the

job of directing attention away from the famil-
iarity of her conversation with Henry. When Mrs
Buckley said she was going to check on her
husband, she made her excuses and followed her
up the stairs to her own room.

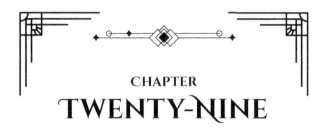

"I can't quite believe all this," Flo said in a quiet voice as the two women vanished at the top of the stairs. George wanted to reach out to her, to take her in an embrace and tell her it was all going to be fine, that he would protect her. Instead, he shuffled nervously and nodded in agreement.

"It's certainly all a bit of a shock."

He looked across at Jessie Circle, who was looking up the stairs with a thoughtful expression, and turned back to Flo.

"Flo, has Henry ever mentioned knowing this Juliet Atoll before?"

She blinked at him for a moment, glanced at

Jessie, whose attention had now returned to their little group, then back to him.

"No, but it appeared he did," she answered in a conspiratorial whisper.

"I would say it's nailed on those two know each other," Jessie added. "The question is, why didn't Henry mention so before? I mean, he's had ample time. We've known Miss Atoll was part of this group since yesterday morning."

"It makes you wonder if everyone here is quite who they seem," Flo said.

"What do you mean?" George asked.

Flo leaned in further, and George felt a small shiver of excitement run down his spine.

"We think that Hove might have been an actor."

"An actor?! You mean just playing the part of the solicitor?"

"Exactly!"

"But," said George, his mind working through the implications of this news, "if he isn't a real lawyer, how do we know that any of this is true? The inheritance, I mean. Is it all some big scam?"

"I don't think it's entirely a scam," Flo answered, her full lips pursed. "I think we were told exactly what we are all doing here up at the standing stones."

"You mean," Jessie said, a note of thrill creeping into her voice, "that we really have been gathered here to find out what happened to your friend Elina?"

"Let's think about it," Flo continued, her eyes darting around as though she was working through an invisible text only she could see. "This group of people were invited here for the express purpose of discovering Elina's killer. This Hove character, or Frank Sparkes as we now know, was the one organising this whole thing, or was hired to pose as a lawyer."

"But why?" Jessie asked. "I mean, if someone had information on Elina's death, they could just take that to the police."

"That's exactly what worries me," Flo said, her face clouding into a deep frown.

"You think this might be someone looking to enact their own sort of justice?" George asked.

"If someone thought that way," Flo said, "what better pretence for gathering this group of strangers together than a large inheritance from a mysterious benefactor?"

"And no real lawyer," Jessie said, picking up on her train of thought, "would ever lower themselves to pretend there was an inheritance where there wasn't one. So they hired an actor to play one and sent out letters to lure us all here."

"But surely, they can't think we had anything to do with Elina's death?" George said, looking at them both in horror.

"No, of course not," Flo said. "Maybe they brought us and Henry here because we were her friends. They might have thought we knew something that could help."

"She's right," Jessie asserted. "Maybe you were brought here as people with a vested interest in bringing her killer to justice."

"Gosh," George said with feeling, "like some band of amateur detectives."

George watched the two women exchange glances, and was surprised to see a hint of excitement playing on their faces rather than the shock he had expected.

He had the rather strange feeling of being left out of some private inside joke.

"Of course," he said, bringing their attention back to him, "this still doesn't explain why Henry knows Miss Atoll and why he hasn't mentioned it."

"No," Flo said, her face turning back to a frown.

A nna closed the bedroom door behind her and leaned against it. Mr Hove, the lawyer, was dead. She did not know what that meant, but something unnerved her more than the death itself.

She looked down at the hulking figure of her husband lying prostrate on the bed, covered so fully in the bedcovers that no part of him was actually visible. The steady rise and fall of the pile, alongside a light snoring, showed he was still asleep. The dose of sleeping powder she had given him last night still had its tight embrace on her husband. He may not wake until lunchtime. The question was, what would she do then?

Her husband was one of those men who had

blundered through life with no foresight or cunning, and had somehow found himself in the enviable position of being a partner in a successful shipping company. Of course, in the latter of this period she had had no small part in guiding his decision-making to bring more prudence, more likely to bring about better results for them both. Maybe that was where it had all started to go wrong, she reflected.

She moved from the door and perched on the edge of the bed, pulling the covers back to reveal Edward's face, slack with unconsciousness, lips slightly parted. She remembered his face each time he had gifted her a new piece of jewellery, every time he had taken them to dinner at the Savoy and enjoyed long, exquisite meals. He had taken such pleasure in providing her with the finer things in life, and she had encouraged him.

At some point, the lavish spending had outweighed the income, and he had taken another route. A route that was sure to lead to their destruction if it hadn't been for the most unfortunate of incidents. Fortunate for them at least, but not for the life that had been lost. The event still hung between them, though. Edward had turned more and more heavily to drink, where he would become maudlin and, worse still, talkative.

She could not allow him to set loose his lips in company such as this. Certainly not with a potential inheritance on the line which would allow them to live their lives in proper comfort once more. She would have to reflect on how to approach the rest of their stay here.

THIRTY-ONE

"When are they going to be here?" Jessie asked, looking over Flo's shoulder.

Flo turned to see the butler, Stammerthwaite, emerge from the small recess in front of the drawing room where the telephone cupboard was located.

"I'm afraid they won't be coming anytime soon, miss," the butler said in his deep, mahogany voice. "Apparently, the storm has caused several trees to fall, one of which has blocked the top road and will take some time to cut and move, even once they can get to it."

"They're not clearing it now?" Flo asked.

"No miss, I'm afraid the conditions on top of the hill are still rather extreme."

"But you told them we have a dead body?" George asked, sounding slightly incredulous at this lack of urgency.

"I did, sir, but the village policeman was of the opinion that if Mr Hove was already dead, he would probably remain so until he could arrive."

Flo let out a long breath. There wasn't much argument there, but it didn't make her feel any easier. If the road was cut off, they were going to all have to spend another night here. Another night of listening to the wind rattling in the loose panes of her bedroom window. This time, though, she would know that not far below here there lay a body, stretched out on the billiard table in the dark.

She shuddered involuntarily.

"Will that be all, miss?" the butler said, as though the death of one of the principal guests of the house was an occurrence as inconvenient as a mere spilled glass of wine.

"Yes, of course," Jessie said distractedly.

The butler shuffled off and the three of them were alone again.

"I don't care if it's still technically morning," Jessie said. "I'm in need of a drink."

"I'm not going to argue," Flo answered.

"I'll join you in a minute," George said as they turned towards the drawing room. "I'm going to ring this village policeman myself and see if I can get any better answer."

"I want you to tell me about Elina," Jessie said as she crossed the drawing room towards the drinks cabinet.

Flo sighed as she dropped into an armchair. It was perfectly reasonable that Jessie would want to know about Elina. Her death was the reason for them all being in this dreary valley. Still, she had to take a moment to steel herself before bringing up the memories of her friend she had increasingly tried to bury. They were too painful.

"She was lively, funny. You would have liked her," Flo said with a sad smile. "She enjoyed her cocktails rather too much as well. She was always flying through life like she didn't have a care in the world."

"What was her background?"

"She was an only child. Her mother died in

childbirth, I'm afraid. Her family had interests in India, but something estranged her from her father..." She trailed off as her train of thought derailed suddenly.

Jessie turned around from where she was preparing gin and tonics.

"What is it?"

Flo closed her eyes and pinched the bridge of her nose.

"I'm an idiot! That's what was bothering me about Mr Badala right from the start!"

"Well?" Jessie asked when Flo had merely stared into the distance for a moment instead of continuing.

Flo opened her mouth to answer, then looked up as the door opened and saw Anna Buckley entering. "Nothing for now," she whispered before turning to the new arrival. "Mrs Buckley, is your husband feeling any better?"

"Yes, thank you. I'm sure he'll be down shortly for lunch."

"Oh good," Flo said, "I must admit that in the current situation, I shall be glad to have some more men around."

Jessie gave a sort of snort at this as she turned back to the drinks cabinet. "Heavens, Flo, we really must try to knock that out of you. The moment you rely on a man for something is the moment you get let down. Isn't that right, Mrs Buckley?"

Anna Buckley had taken a seat near Flo, perched on a wingback armchair like a small bird.

"Men have their uses," she replied primly, before looking slightly shocked as Jessie approached and shoved a cocktail glass in her hand.

"Oh, I'm not denying that," Jessie said with a sly smile. "I've made use of them myself often enough."

Flo felt her cheeks flush at this comment as Jessie handed her the drink with a wink.

"So," Jessie continued into what now seemed a rather embarrassed silence, "how did you and your husband know Elina Fortesque, and what reason could you have had to murder her?"

Jessie picked up her own drink and smiled at Anna Buckley as calmly as though she had asked her to share where she had bought her dress.

Flo found she was gripping her glass so hard her knuckles were white.

Anna Buckley remained immovable, the sharp lines of her face and her pursed lips like some porcelain figure. When she spoke, it was with a calm resignation, as though she had just decided on a course of action she found inevitable and tiresome.

"I see you have come to the same conclusion I have, Miss Circle. Clearly, as the unfortunate man currently lying in the billiard room said, we have been gathered here to discover the facts of the murder of Miss Elina Fortesque. Therefore, each of us must have had some reason to have wanted the woman dead."

"Except me," Jessie smiled, "they did not invite me."

"And yet," Anna said with a thin smile, "here you are."

"Quite so." Jessie nodded. "So, how about we get the ball rolling with hearing why you wanted her dead?"

"Maybe Miss Hammond would like to go first?" Mrs Buckley said, her eyes fixing on Flo with a hard stare.

"I...I..." Flo floundered before Jessie cut in.

"Oh, that's easy," she said before taking a sip of her drink. "Flo here is an absolute sweetheart, but she needs to come out of herself and stop behaving like a cancelled stamp. From what I've heard, Elina was more of an outgoing party girl.

Maybe Flo was jealous of this easygoing attitude. One day she couldn't take any more and bumped her off." She turned to Flo. "How did she die, by the way?"

Flo was too shocked and horrified by this sudden accusation against her to speak. Instead, she gaped at Jessie as though she had slapped her.

"Oh, don't be silly, Flo. I know you didn't murder her. I was just establishing your motive. Now come on, how did she die?"

"They bludgeoned her over the head," Anna Buckley answered before Flo could regain her composure.

"Ah!" Jessie said. "So you know of the case?"

"It was in the London papers," Anna replied flatly.

"Of course," Jessie said thoughtfully.

The door opened and George came in, shaking his head.

"No more luck with the local bobby than Stammerthwaite had," he said. "They don't think the road will be clear until tomorrow afternoon at the earliest."

"What's this?" Anna said, her head swinging round to him and then back to Jessie.

"We were hoping the police could come and

deal with our situation in the billiard room," she said, her eyes narrowed.

Flo blinked, marvelling at her ability to talk of the corpse on the games table as she might a deep tear in its felt.

"Presumably the police would also look into the rather curious situation we all find ourselves in here?" Anna Buckley said.

"Damn, you're right," George said in irritation. "I didn't mention that on the phone. I mean, he already knew we were here for a will reading and I said the whole thing seemed a bit fishy, but I didn't tell him what Hove had said at the standing stones. Not that it would have made much difference in how fast he could have got here, I suppose."

Henry paused with his hand on the doorknob to the drawing room. He hadn't planned on this, hadn't in his wildest nightmares foreseen it, but matters were what they were. He needed someone on his side. Someone who could see the difficult situation he was in and help him navigate it. Unfortunately, there was only one proper candidate.

He took a deep breath and opened the door.

All four sets of eyes turned to him as he came in, and he had the vague feeling that he had interrupted something.

"I'm sorry," he stammered on instinct, but then realised he did, in fact, owe the group an apology. "I'm sorry for my behaviour earlier. It was uncalled for." He turned his eyes from the ladies to George. "I wondered if I could have a word in private, George?"

George's face did its usual, gaping, idiotic look as it glanced around the women of the room before answering.

"Right, yes. Of course," he said as he headed towards Henry and the door.

They made their way out into the hall and across to the library. Once inside, they moved right into a small study that Stammerthwaite had called 'the business room' when he had shown him earlier.

He shut the door behind them and perched on the edge of the solid oak desk that dominated the room. George stood awkwardly by the door, looking slightly nervous.

"Sit down, for heaven's sake," Henry said, gesturing at the chair in front of him. George fell into it in a shot, and Henry inwardly cursed himself for his shortness.

George had always had this effect on him. An ability to bring out his snide, petty side. The man just annoyed him so much! His awkwardness at every aspect of life, the adoring puppy eyes the size of dinner plates behind his thick-lensed glasses every time he looked at Flo. He was pathetic.

Right now, though, he needed him.

"Look, old chap," he began in a more friendly tone. "I know I like to rib you occasionally and all that, but I consider you a good friend."

"Oh, right," George answered in surprise.

"It's just," Henry continued, trying to find the right way of saying what he needed to. "I'm in a bit of a fix here, and I could do with someone on my side."

George's eyes went wide. "Did you kill the lawyer?!"

"No! Damn it, George, of course not."

"Oh..." George blew out his cheeks with apparent relief.

Henry took a deep breath, already half regretting his decision to bring George into his confidence.

"Look, you probably saw from that brief episode with Juliet that we're not exactly strangers."

"Yes, the others thought that."

"Others?"

"Flo and Jessie."

"Oh, right?" Henry nodded to himself. This

was what he had been worried about. He shouldn't be surprised that the thought had already occurred to some.

"Well, the fact is, we do know each other. Have done for years."

"You've never mentioned her?"

"No, and there's a reason for that."

Henry closed his eyes. This was it, the moment where he would reveal the secret he had held on to for so long now.

"Juliet and I were very close when we were younger, before the war."

"Close?" George asked, his tone implying he had grasped the meaning behind this simple word.

"Yes," Henry continued, his voice breaking slightly. He cleared it and continued. "We were going to be married, then of course I went off to fight. You know what happened to me, of course."

George nodded. "Shrapnel in the leg."

"Yes, kept me in a field hospital for quite a time, and it was clear I wouldn't be going back to the front any time soon. Things were chaotic then, and I ended up limping around the hospital helping where I could, instead of coming back."

"Very admirable," George said.

Henry gave a snort. "Foolish was what it was. When I did finally get back, I found that, through some mix-up, they had declared me missing in action. Juliet, understandably, had moved on."

"Moved on...?" George asked.

Henry sighed again. "She's always been beautiful. She had a poise and grace about her even when she was just a girl of ten. She lived with her grandmother then. She never knew what happened to her parents. Both dead, I assume. She used to joke that she was the illegitimate daughter of aristocracy. The way she carried herself, even then, you could half believe it."

George moved in his chair, and Henry was torn from his thoughts about the past. He took a deep breath.

"When I came back, she was moving in different circles. It seems that beauty and grace go a long way in determining one's social position."

"And now she's engaged to some lord or other?" George asked.

"Yes, Lord Perciville Baxter," Henry answered, not needing to feign the bitter taste of that name in his mouth. "A lecherous old salt, retired from the navy. Twice her age."

"Good lord!" George exclaimed. "I can see why

this entire business must be damn awkward, but dash it. Why haven't you mentioned her before?"

"I was trying to move on. Trying to forget it all."

"And then she turns up here, of all places! But what connection could she have to Elina?"

"None at all," Henry answered quickly. Too quickly, he realised. George was looking at him with a slight frown, which meant the idiot was thinking for once. "I just mean, how can she have? Juliet and I were all over years ago."

"Yes, of course," George said, but Henry noticed the frown remained.

Before he could steer the subject to safer waters, a woman's scream made its way through the thick door of the business room.

For a moment they simply stared at each other, too dumbfounded to speak, to move even.

"What?" George said, in that infuriatingly feeble way of his, which had the invigorating effect of snapping Henry to his senses. He jumped up and charged through the door, into the library, and then out into the hall.

Flo and Jessie had already emerged from the drawing room, wide-eyed and staring at him with a mixture of horror and excitement. He realised, even amid this adrenaline-fueled moment, that it was excitement he noticed more of in both their expressions.

Another female wail of despair dragged their gazes towards the discreet baize door which hid in the room's corner.

"It's coming from the servants' quarters," he said, realising his words were idiotic as he said them. As though behind that door lay a different world, which in some ways, he supposed it did.

He moved towards it, the others close behind. As the door swung open noiselessly at his touch, it revealed the crumpled figure of Stammerthwaite at the bottom of the servants' stairs in front of them. To the left, Juliet's maid was being consoled by an older woman. As the maid turned to the door, her eyes locked on his and he saw them widen in terror. She screamed again before hurrying away.

THIRTY-THREE

lo sipped at her tea as she studied the young woman's face opposite her. She had a round, pleasant face. Not overly beautiful as such, but soft and kind. Right now, it was pinched with fear. Flo realised that it had been ever since she had first seen her back at the Red Lion, which already seemed like an age ago.

"Now, are you feeling a little better?" Jessie said softly, placing her hand on top of the girl's and squeezing it. The girl nodded, but she certainly didn't look any better.

She had been in a fit of near hysterics since discovering the crumpled form of the butler at the bottom of the stairs. He was alive, there was that at least, and had been taken to the butler's pantry.

He was laid out on the floor there, with Henry attending him, assisted by George. Henry was the only person in the house with any medical experience.

At the maid's screams, everyone had come running apart from Edward Buckley, who was still apparently confined to his room. Jessie had taken charge, a role Flo was realising came naturally to her. They had ushered everyone from the kitchen where the maid was recovering, including Juliet, who seemed to have created as much fear in the young girl as their appearance at the scene of the incident had.

"Your name's Kate, isn't it?" Jessie asked.

The maid took a sip of her highly sugared tea before replying.

"Yes, miss. Kate Fielding."

"OK then, Kate, why don't you tell us what happened?"

She nodded and swallowed before speaking.

"Miss Atoll was...," she paused and looked at them both, "a bit upset, and so I was coming to get her a glass of brandy. I took the servants' stairs, and that's when I found him."

"And did you see anyone else when you left

Miss Atoll's room and came to the stairs?" Jessie asked.

"No, no one."

Flo saw the disappointment written on Jessie's face.

"Did you hear him cry out at all?" she asked hopefully.

"No, sorry, nothing."

Flo knew she had to ask. She knew she could never get that look of pure terror out of her mind, the one she had seen on the girl when Henry had come in the door, without asking.

"Kate," she said gently, "do you know Henry Bitten?"

The reaction was immediate and physical. The young woman shuddered into more sobs, but this time her eyes were wide in fear, her head shaking back and forth as though she had been offered something unpleasant at dinner and was refusing emphatically.

"Oh lord help me, I don't know what's going on!" she cried suddenly, her fists clenching. "I don't understand why I'm here, why he's here!"

"You mean Henry Bitten, don't you?" Flo said.

The young woman looked up with wet, sad eyes. "It's not my place to say anything, miss."

Flo nodded slowly. "You said last night that you had received a letter to come here. Did you know Elina Fortesque?"

Kate Fielding bit her bottom lip and looked down as she twisted the sodden hanky in her hands.

"I knew her, miss, but I don't want to talk about it."

"I don't know if you know what's going on here Kate," Jessie said in a soft voice, "but there's no point in keeping secrets now. We're all in this together, and the sooner we find out exactly what's going on, the sooner we can all get out of here."

The woman's face tightened while taking a deep breath as though gathering her resolve.

"I'm not going to say any more."

Flo thought for a moment and changed tack. She turned to Jessie.

"I think we should talk to Miss Atoll and see if she can think of any reason Miss Fielding here would know Elina, don't you?"

"No!" Kate cried before Jessie could answer.

Flo and Jessie exchanged a look.

"Are you afraid of her?" Flo asked.

"It just all seems to be coming together and I don't know what that means, but it scares me!"

"What's coming together?!" Flo asked, exasperated, surprising herself at her forcefulness.

"Oh god," Kate said, "I swear I didn't know anything bad would happen to her! I didn't think Miss Atoll could have had anything to do with it, but then that man. Those dark eyes of his. I started to wonder and then I thought, 'what if it was all because of me? What if I got her killed?!'"

She was hysterical again now and shaking with either the sobbing or fear, Flo couldn't tell.

The door to the kitchen opened, and George appeared, looking red and flustered.

"I'm sorry," he said nervously, looking between the three women, "but something very odd has happened."

Flo exchanged looks with Jessie. She could tell from her frown that she was just as reluctant to leave this interview as Flo was, but the sense of urgent confusion in George's voice made them silently decide.

"You just wait here for a minute, Kate," Flo said, patting her on the arm. "We'll be right back."

The girl nodded before blowing her nose

noisily as they left the kitchen and headed across the servants' hall to the butler's pantry.

"What exactly?" Jessie began before stopping short as she looked down at the stricken form of the butler.

"Where on earth is his beard?!" she exclaimed.

Which was exactly what Flo had been thinking. The man lying on the carpet seemed transformed. His eye patch was gone, which Flo assumed Henry had done while checking his injuries, and the eye showed no sign of injury or abnormality. This, though, was nothing to the completely clean-shaven jaw of the man. The large bushy beard he had been sporting was gone, and instead, a rather weak, dimpled chin remained.

"It was false," Henry said. "I'm pretty sure there's nothing wrong with his eye, either." He was fiddling around at the side of the man's head and suddenly pulled back what appeared to be the man's scalp. George gave a small cry of astonishment next to her as a bald dome was revealed from under the wig that Henry now lifted away.

"The man will live," Henry said after a period of stunned silence, "whoever he is. I don't want to move him upstairs to his room, so we'll need to set up a makeshift bed here."

Flo looked at the unconscious man, so trans-formed from the grizzled appearance he had had such a short time ago. Without the beard, the long hair and the eye patch, he cut a much more normal figure. A balding man in his early sixties, she would guess. His somewhat swarthy complexion remained, pointing to a life lived mostly outdoors or in hotter climes.

"Will he need supervision?" Jessie asked.

"He needs medical attention," Henry said, standing up with a sigh, "but until we can get him that, we just need to wait until he wakes. No idea when that will be."

A muffled cry from somewhere far away in the house caused everyone in the room to stiffen at once. Flo turned towards Jessie, who was already heading for the door.

J uliet lay on her bed, staring up at the myriad of hairline cracks which ran from the wall above her bed. They spread out from a central line like branches from a tree.

She thought of Elina Fortesque. She was the cause of all this tension between her and Henry. She was the reason everyone was here, in this house.

She sat upright and cursed. Where was Kate with her drink? She would have to go downstairs herself and find one for herself and just do her best to avoid Henry. She rose from the bed and then froze. The scream sent a bolt of fear down her spine that seemed to have frozen her muscles temporarily.

The second scream broke the spell, and she pulled her bedroom door open and turned to her left as the cry faded into a sob.

Anna Buckley was standing, her hands at her mouth, trudging backwards. She ran to her, her bare feet making the ancient floorboards creak as each foot landed.

She slowed to a stop as she reached the pitiful sight of Anna Buckley. No tears were present on her ghostly pale cheeks. Her eyes, wide and unblinking, stared back towards the open door of her room.

Juliet had never been the most tactful of people, but she knew the women needed comforting. She put her arms around her awkwardly as she saw the rest of the house party emerge from the stairs.

THIRTY-FIVE

H enry ran to Juliet as soon as he saw her.

"Are you all right?" he asked, his voice sounding desperate and panicked even to his own ears.

"I'm fine," she replied in a small, distant voice. "It's Mrs Buckley, I... I think something's happened."

Henry looked at Anna Buckley, who was shaking, her eyes wide.

"Good Lord!" George said, making him turn around.

The others had moved to the Buckleys' bedroom door, which remained open. He left Juliet and moved across to it, pushing past George to enter the room.

Edward Buckley lay on the bed, his lifeless eyes staring up at the ceiling, his pillow stood up against the headboard behind him.

"He's dead," Flo said pointlessly.

Henry felt his stomach clench. Things were wrong here, very wrong indeed.

He hurried to the side of the bed and felt the man's pulse, even though he knew it was useless.

"He's warm to the touch, he hasn't been dead long." he said as he watched Jessie Circle pick up a small glass bottle from the side table opposite.

"Sleeping pills," she said.

"You don't think he...?" Flo said before trailing off, but the implication was clear.

"The man's overweight," Henry said. "He clearly liked his drink. Maybe his heart wasn't in the best of health?"

Henry reached out to close the man's eyes. He couldn't take their empty, soulless stare anymore.

"Wait," Flo said, holding her hand out in a gesture that stopped his arm in mid-air. She leaned down over Edward Buckley's face, her eyes narrowed in concentration.

Henry glanced at Jessie on the other side of the bed and then at George, who was still by the door. Both seemed as confused as he was as he watched the

"What is it?" Jessie said eventually from her side.

"His eyes," Flo said, "look."

Jessie leaned over next to her, and Henry followed suit from the other side.

Edward Buckley's eyes were severely blood-shot, almost to where there was no longer any white to be seen in them. Henry frowned with a mixture of curiosity and rising dread. He couldn't remember ever seeing eyes like that on the battle-field, and he'd seen his fair share of eye injuries.

"The eyes go like that when someone's been suffocated," Flo said bluntly. "Look at the position of the pillow," she continued, gesturing at the upright object behind the deceased's head. "He's not lying on it. I think someone has taken it from under his head and smothered him with it."

Jessie looked at her curiously.

"That previous case I was involved in," Flo explained, "asphyxiation."

Jessie nodded, her eyes seemingly scrutinising Flo anew.

"He would have woken up, surely?" George said from the doorway.

"Not if he'd taken these," Jessie said, removing her gaze from Flo and shaking the pill box she still held. "I think we should go to the drawing room. It's time for people to lay their cards on the table."

THIRTY-SIX

Anna took the brandy Jessie offered her and took a deep sip. The burn of the fiery liquid down her throat didn't seem to be real. Nothing did.

Edward was dead.

She couldn't think of anything beyond that at the moment, but she knew she had to. She needed to get her head clear, now more than ever.

She felt a wave of panic. She had killed her husband. She could hang for this.

She swallowed the bile that was rising in her throat.

"Now," Jessie Circle said as paced up and down in the middle of the room.

The American had gathered them all in the

drawing room while Flo Hammond, who seemed permanently at her side, had supplied drinks.

"Since we've been in this house, a man has fallen to his death from his bedroom window and the butler has fallen down the service stairs." The American paused at the far end of the room and looked around her audience.

"Both men appear to have not been who they said they were. Our legal representative appears to have been an actor playing a role, and the butler was wearing a false beard and hairpiece. I think it's fair to assume there is a lot more to our little weekend away here than any of us first thought. I'm sorry to do this, Mrs Buckley, but I think we should start with you and what happened to your husband."

Anna lifted her chin, ready to launch a fiery rebuke at her questioner, but as she looked into those grey eyes... something in her gave way. There was no malice there, nothing accusatory. The woman was looking at her in pity.

For years, Anna had been pushing for them to have a better life. She had wanted respect, respect only money could bring. She knew people in the higher circles had sneered at them behind their backs, but she was determined. Then it had all gone so horribly wrong, and their desperate need to save face had led them to not a financial ruin, but a ruin of the soul.

Her shoulders slumped. She was tired. Tired of it all, and now Edward was gone. What was the use of the hard shell she had created around herself now? How could anything protect her anymore?

Perhaps sensing this change in her, the American continued.

"Was Edward using the sleeping draught that was next to the bed?" Jessie asked.

Anna answered without raising her head.

"No, that is mine. I have always suffered bouts of insomnia, and so keep it with me. Today I gave Edward some in order to make him sleep through the day."

Anna could feel the silence in the room increase in pressure. Everyone was now judging her actions. She lifted her head and met each of their gazes. It was time.

"Edward was a bullheaded, obstinate man," she began. Her voice shook slightly before finding its normal tone. "But he was a decent one. He worked hard to make our lives more comfortable." She paused and took a deep breath in. "But I pushed him every day. I wanted him to strive for more, always more. Everything was going as I had hoped. We seemed to have more money and more status with every passing year. That was what I wanted, of course—status." She gave a humourless laugh. "I was such a fool."

"I'm sorry," Henry Bitten said, his arrogant face fixed on her. "What exactly does all this have to do with today's events?"

"Miss Circle here has already given her opinion that this is no ordinary weekend invitation," Anna answered, feeling some of her old fire returning. "I am explaining the reason I believe my husband and I came to be here."

At the mention of Edward, she felt the strength in her fade again, and she took another long sip of brandy.

"Please, go on, Mrs Buckley," Jessie whispered.

"Edward began drinking more," she continued after a moment. "His mood became more erratic and unpredictable. I knew something was wrong, but he would brush me off whenever I asked. Then Cedric died."

She looked up at the blank expressions around the room.

"Cedric Baxter was Edward's partner. Together

they ran the Eastwood shipping company."

"Of course!" Henry exclaimed. "I thought I'd heard the name Edward Buckley. The whole thing collapsed, with a lot of company funds missing. It was all over the papers."

"Yes, I'm afraid it was," Anna cut in, giving the young man a sharp look.

The whole thing still felt like a raw wound in her stomach that would never heal. A sense of shame and fear that she knew would be with her forever, no matter how hard she tried to bury it. She sat up a little straighter and took a deep breath, steadying herself.

"I'm afraid Edward was too trusting. The company seemed to have some difficulties with cash flow, but they assured him it was just a temporary issue. He had rather a lot of faith in Cedric, you see. Then Cedric died suddenly and things began to unravel."

"How did this Cedric chap die?" George asked.

Anna looked at him sharply. "There was nothing suspicious about his death, if that's what you are insinuating!"

"No!" George exclaimed before spluttering an apology.

Anna looked down her nose at him, feeling

buoyed by still being able to get a physical response from a tongue lashing.

"After Cedric had died," she continued, her voice stronger now, "it was discovered that there was a large amount of money missing from the company that could not be explained. It was clear that the man had been leeching off of the company for many years."

"And the company ended up being sold off piecemeal to some American company, as I remember," Henry added. "But I'm sorry, I still don't understand what this has to do with anything."

"Elina Fortesque," Anna spat the name as though it was poison, which in her mind it was. "When I heard that blasted name in the stone circle, I should have left immediately. She came to us and said she had proof that it had been Edward who had taken the company money. Even had the gall to suggest that Cedric's death was on the hands of Edward."

"I don't believe it," Flo said.

Anna looked at the girl coldly. A slip of a thing with her frizzy blonde hair and baby blue eyes. What would she know about judging someone's character? What would she know about life at all?!

"I think it's clear that you didn't know your friend as well as you think you did," she said, smiling slightly as a pained look crossed the silly girl's face. "She was a filthy blackmailer out to make a grubby living from respectable people."

For a moment, Anna thought the girl would argue back, but then she saw a thoughtful, confused look pass across her face and she turned away.

Anna folded her arms with a self-satisfied smile until she turned again to Miss Circle, who was glaring at her with an intensity that unnerved her. The thought of Edward lying dead in the bed upstairs, and with it, the image of the hangman's noose returned to her.

"I didn't poison my husband," she found herself saying as she looked into those accusing grey eyes.

"I know you didn't," Flo replied.

Anna turned and blinked at her for a moment, a mix of relief and confusion washing over her.

"The sleeping draught," was all she managed to say, her throat dry.

Flo looked back at her, feeling as though her mind was clearing suddenly.

"You administered it to him without his knowledge, am I correct?"

Anna opened her mouth, but her throat had become dry and unmoving.

"I think," Flo continued, rising from her chair now and moving to stand by Jessie, "that you intentionally drugged your husband in order to keep him quiet. We have all arrived here to find one or more of us, accused of involvement in a murder. I believe you when you say that Elina Fortesque was blackmailing you and your husband."

Everyone, like Anna, was transfixed on her. Strangely, Flo realised that instead of the normal feeling of her cheeks becoming hot and a strange desire to run through the nearest exit, she was enjoying it.

"In fact," she realised with a sudden sick feeling in her stomach, "I suspect that Elina Fortesque is likely to have been blackmailing everyone invited here this weekend."

There was a mix of muttered curse words and sharp intakes of breath at this.

"No!" George cried.

"I'm sorry, George, but I think so. Elina had no job, no income. Her father had cut her off. She was secretive and evasive. We've all said it before. Elina was a mystery, and this goes some way to explaining why."

She turned back to Anna now, who felt herself almost recoil under the intensity of the gaze.

"I don't know if you or your husband killed his business partner, but I think Elina had something over you and was blackmailing you because of it." She turned and looked around the room. "Yesterday we were treated to a rather theatrical display up at the standing stones. I say theatrical, because that was how it felt at the time, but also because we now know it was exactly that. The late Mr Hove gave us the ominous task of uncovering a murderer, but he was no more a solicitor than I am a nun. He was an actor, presumably paid to put on this charade to frighten us, which explains why we were marched up to the standing stones. The more drama, the more intimidation. We only discovered this, however, after he had died, fallen, or pushed, from his bedroom window."

She placed her hands on her hips and looked at her silent audience, each in turn.

"We've been given the task of discovering a murderer, and I am now convinced there is one here to be discovered."

CHAPTER

THIRTY-SEVEN

F lo's fists were curled into balls at her side as she looked around the room. Everyone was now doing the same. Sizing each other up. Trying to determine if there really could be a killer in their midst.

Her own eye finally came to rest on Jessie Circle, who was making no effort whatsoever to disguise the look of pure excitement on her face.

What Flo felt then was mostly a sense of shock. Until the moment she had declared her old friend a blackmailer, she wasn't aware that she had even considered the idea. Then, as soon as the words had left her lips, suddenly things had made sense.

Elina had always been evasive of how she

funded her lifestyle, one that was beyond Flo's means, despite her steady income from the newspaper. Elina had had no work that Flo knew of, despite her probing, but there was money. There always seemed to be money. Cash in irregular bursts to be squandered in the jazz clubs of the capital that she had loved so much.

Elina had never blackmailed her. She had been her friend. Or was it simply that Flo's rather dull life had never created a situation for Flo to be blackmailed about?

She looked up at George and Henry. She was sure Elina hadn't blackmailed them, either. The four of them got on. Someone had clearly blackmailed the Buckleys. The ferocity of Anna Buckley's comments left her in no doubt that, she at least, thought Elina was responsible. That left only two people at the house who had both claimed they had never known Elina. Jessie Circle and Juliet Atoll.

Juliet had apparently received an invitation to the will reading, just as everyone else had. Her maid, though, had also received an invitation, which was most curious. The young woman seemed to know Elina as well.

Jessie was the only one who hadn't. Instead,

she had just happened to be at the inn the entire gathering had been staying at. Flo had thought it was her that had invited the American, but now she looked back on her first few meetings with the woman, it was clear she had virtually invited herself.

Her train of thought was derailed by Anna Buckley.

"You said you knew I didn't kill my husband," she said in a quiet voice. Flo considered it remarkable how much the woman's demeanour had changed in the past few minutes.

"I did," she replied with a confidence she didn't entirely feel. "If you regularly take a sleeping draught, I would imagine you have a good sign of what dosage is required. I would also suggest that it would be an idiotic way of killing your husband, as someone would clearly point the finger at you. No, you didn't murder your husband, Mrs Buckley, but I'm afraid you gave the opportunity to someone else." She took a deep breath and looked at Anna Buckley with a frown. "I apologise if what I am about to say is upsetting for you," she said softly, "but I'm afraid from the severely bloodshot eyes your husband had after death, I would say it's likely someone smothered him."

For a moment, the room was so still it felt to Flo as though the very air had been sucked from the space. She gathered herself to say the terrible thought that had been growing silently at the back of her mind like a poisonous weed.

"I think," she said hurriedly, before the courage to say it left her, "that whoever gathered you all here this weekend did so because they believed one of you had murdered her, and they seek revenge."

"My god," Anna Buckley murmured, the colour draining from her face.

"So this person you allude to who invited us all here, apparently under false pretences," Juliet Atoll said, speaking for the first time since they had entered the room, "presumably discovered Mr Buckley was responsible for the murder of this Elina Fortesque, and in return murdered him in revenge?"

"No," Jessie said.

Flo looked up at her, the woman's face alive with the glow of excitement.

"That wouldn't explain things," the American continued. "If Flo is right, and they have brought us here to find out what happened to Elina, then it's safe to say whoever arranged this didn't know for sure. They must have discovered that she was blackmailing people, and gathered them here to determine the truth."

"And as I said," Juliet replied, "they discovered it was Edward Buckley and murdered him!"

"My husband did not kill anybody!" Anna Buckley said sharply.

"It is clear," Flo continued, her own voice growing loud to stop any further comments, "that even if Mr Buckley was the person responsible for Elina's death, then we now have another killer at the house. Someone bent on revenge."

There was a moment of silence before George finally broke the tension.

"If that's the case, then it's all over," he said in a shaky voice. "This person has got their revenge or whatever."

"Once the road is passable, we can let the police decide who's responsible," Henry said, nodding in agreement.

"And in the meantime, we're supposed to just stay here knowing that there's a murderer under the roof?" Juliet said in a sharp tone directed at Henry.

"I don't see that we have any other choice," Henry answered quietly.

"There is of course another possibility," Jessie said, her grey eyes still wide and alive with excitement. "The killer might not know the identity of the person who murdered Elina Fortesque, and has decided simply to gather the people considered most likely, and kill them all to ensure they have found their target. I think everyone in this room should consider whether they want to reveal that they were being blackmailed by Elina. It seems likely to me that whoever the killer is, they would be the one person not being blackmailed by Elina."

"I can tell you right now that I wasn't," Flo said fiercely, causing the corners of Jessie's wide mouth to turn up briefly.

"Nor me," George said.

"Or me," Henry added.

"Then I think it's safe to say that you three are our chief suspects," Jessie said with a smile, turning to Juliet Atoll before any of them could respond. "And you, Miss Atoll? Were you being blackmailed by Elina Fortesque?"

The slender, elegant form of Juliet straightened in her chair before placing her hands on her lap and looking into Jessie's eyes.

"As a matter of fact, I was."

Flo watched the woman's eyes flicker across the room, pausing for a moment, then returning to Jessie.

"I don't suppose you'd like to explain to us exactly what she was blackmailing you over?" Jessie asked.

"No, I would not... like to," Juliet answered icily, "but I will."

"Juliet!" Henry said, jumping upright in his seat in alarm.

"Please be quiet, Henry," Juliet snapped. "I'm quite capable of speaking for myself."

Flo watched Henry's mouth open, then close again, before he stood up and stalked over to the drinks cabinet.

As the silence spread out, Flo found herself clearing her throat to speak.

"I think it is clear that the two of you know each other. Let us save that for a little later and first, tell us why you were being blackmailed." She turned to scan the rest of the people in the room. "And I would suggest that once Miss Atoll is done, that anyone else who was blackmailed by Elina should also speak up. The simple reason being that if you are honest and declare what was happening, we can make a pact here and now that nothing of what is said ever leaves this house. Also, if blackmail was the motive for the murder of Elina, disclosing you were being blackmailed here shows you are not so concerned by people hearing the fact, that you would murder to keep the secret."

"That's great!" Jessie exclaimed with wide-eyed astonishment. "Gee Flo, you're a regular fire-cracker when you get going!"

Flo immediately felt her cheeks flush, and she turned away from the American, moving to the edge of the room. She leaned on the wall and tried to slow her breathing with long, deep breaths.

THIRTY-EIGHT

H enry finished speaking and gave a meaningful glance at Juliet.

He had jumped in and offered to explain how they knew each other before she could, and then repeated the story he had told George. It was close enough to the truth to be believable.

"It doesn't seem to be much to blackmail someone over," Jessie said with disappointment.

"It would have ended my engagement," Juliet said with a shrug.

Henry looked up at Flo, who was staring at him from the other side of the room with an intensity in her light blue eyes that was making him uncomfortable.

"It's quite a coincidence, isn't it?" she said, moving away from the wall and stepping towards him.

"What is?" he said.

"That the person blackmailing your old flame just also happened to be a friend of yours? Someone that you regularly spent time with in London?"

"Good lord!" George said, looking at Henry in astonishment. "You were giving Elina information on this lady to blackmail her?"

"No!" Henry protested forcefully. "I would never do that!" He could feel his face reddening as Flo took another step towards him, her eyes blazing with anger.

"In that case," she said in a low, even tone, "the only other explanation is that you knew Miss Atoll was being blackmailed and sought out Elina to stop her."

Henry took in a sharp, involuntary breath, and cursed himself inwardly as he saw recognition in Flo's face that her comment had struck home.

"Is that what happened?" Her anger now mixed with emotion as her voice cracked and her eyes filled with tears. "You joined our little group so you could size up the woman who was blackmailing you. Maybe you planned to persuade her to stop? Maybe you planned to pay her off? Whatever your intentions, I think it's clear what ultimate decision you made. You murdered her in cold blood."

"Flo," Henry said, his voice suddenly hoarse.

Whatever his reasons for joining the small group of Elina Fortesque, Flo Hammond and George Wilson as he did just under a year ago, he had grown to like them. Like them immensely.

Flo was intelligent, and despite her shy nature, she had a strength of will that he had rarely seen in anyone.

Elina had been fun, always fun, with a sharp wit and a wry smile. In another life, he could have even fallen for her.

George was a bumbling idiot who couldn't have found his arse with both hands, but he was a good sort when you got down to it.

He felt a deep pang of shame. What had he done?

"Henry didn't kill Elina!" Juliet said with a sudden fury as she rose from her chair. "We just wanted to find out why she was doing this to us! To reason with her!"

"And this took months?" Flo said incredulously. "You seemed to enjoy yourself in that time, I must say."

"Flo," Henry said again, having regained some composure. He stood and looked her in the eye. "I'm sorry I lied to you," he turned to George, "to all of you, but I didn't know what to do! I was doing what I thought was best for Juliet," he said with feeling.

Juliet moved across to him, her elegant figure gliding across the floor with her eyes locked on Henry's. He took her in his arms, not caring that there were people watching them. Suddenly, none of that seemed important. She bent her forehead to rest against his, as he closed his eyes.

He would love this woman until the day he died.

"It's pretty clear," Jessie said, "that things aren't exactly in the past between you two."

"Oh my god," Flo said, her hand moving to her lips. "This wasn't about saving Juliet's marriage plans, was it? Your plans went further than that."

Henry felt Juliet tense in his arms as a chill ran down his own neck.

"What do you mean?" Jessie said, turning to her with a quizzical expression.

"Think about it," Flo said. "Clearly, these two

are still in love, so why would they possibly care if Juliet's engagement was called off? Wouldn't that mean they could be together? For that matter, why didn't she call it off as soon as Henry had returned from the war and she realised he was alive?"

Jessie's eyes widened, and Henry saw she had realised the truth. He let out a breath that he felt he had been holding for years.

"Can someone fill me in?" George said, blinking behind his thick glasses.

"So," Jessie said, turning back to the couple, "let me guess. Your first reaction to discovering Henry here was alive was for you to break off the engagement. What then, though? Two young people having to start from scratch in the world. I wonder which one of you thought of it first?" she said, raising one eyebrow. "How old is Lord Perciville Baxter?" she asked, looking at Juliet. "Your fiancé must be in his late sixties, and I'm sure I read that there had been some heart issues? You are both young, you have all the time in the world. Certainly enough to bide your time until you are married and your new husband's age and poor health catch up with him. Then, after a suit-able period of public mourning, Lady Baxter would be able to look for love again in the eyes of the world."

"Good lord," George exclaimed.

"And the long-estranged lovers," Jessie continued, "who had, I'm sure, been seeing each other the entire time, could be reunited officially."

"That's the real reason Elina was blackmailing you," Flo said. "She knew exactly what you had planned."

She had said this with her eyes not on Henry or Juliet, but unfocused, with brow furrowed. As though lost in thought.

He looked at Juliet and decided it was time he got her out of this toxic room, even if they couldn't yet leave the godforsaken house. He took her decisively by the arm and headed for the hallway.

Flo watched Henry and Juliet leave as she raised her hands to rub at her temples.

So much had happened in such a brief space of time that she was having trouble processing it all.

Elina was a blackmailer; that was now clear, despite Flo having difficulty matching this to the image she had of her friend. She struggled to think of Elina as someone who could be so callous, so cruel. She had never been that way with her.

With Henry, it was somehow different. She was very clear about how she felt about him right now. Angry. He had lied his way into all of their lives and had done so, not for Juliet's honour or even for love. He had done it simply for greed.

"I think," Anna Buckley said, rising from her chair slightly unsteadily and heading towards the door, "that I might go and lie down for a while..." She paused, frowning.

Flo realised what had occurred to her. Her husband's dead body was still in her room.

"Perhaps we could ask the maid to make up Mr Hove's room fresh for you?" she blurted. "Jessie, maybe you could make Mrs Buckley a drink while I go and arrange it?"

Jessie nodded at her and guided Anna towards the drinks cabinet.

"Can I do anything?" George asked eagerly as he leapt up from his chair.

Flo smiled at him. "Thank you, George, just some moral support is nice at the moment."

He gave a shy smile and his hand reached out to rest on her arm.

"I'll always be here for you, Flo," he said.

There was a moment of silence between them, where Flo was sure he was going to say something else. Then, he pulled his hand away as though he had touched a flame. His cheeks reddened as he stammered something about finding the maid and moved towards the door.

Flo took a moment to compose herself before following him out into the hallway.

George paused as the baize door which led through to the servants' area swung open silently before he could reach it. Juliet's maid Kate appeared and jumped back in shock as she almost collided with George.

"Oh, I'm sorry!" he exclaimed. "I was looking for the parlour maid?"

"She's back in the scullery, sir," the young woman answered nervously. "Would you like me to get her for you?"

"Oh no, it's quite all right," George said, flashing a grin back towards Flo as he vanished through the green door.

Kate Fielding was heading towards the dining room when Flo called out to her, making her freckled, round face turn back to her.

"Yes, miss?" she said, with that same frightened look she'd had since Flo had first seen her back in the Red Lion pub.

"I wondered if I could have a quick word with you?" Flo said, talking in a low, calming voice that she hoped would reassure the girl.

"I need to find Miss Atoll. She often likes a cup

of cocoa before bedtime and she's had such a shock as it is and..."

"Miss Atoll is fine," Flo said, breaking her off before she wittered on all night. "She's speaking with Mr Bitten privately."

Flo was waiting for a reaction, and got one immediately. The girl's eyes widened, one hand moving to her chest.

"Come with me," Flo said, putting her arm around the girl and leading her to the small flower room at the back of the hall.

There were no flowers there now, but the small room still seemed to hold the scent of them faintly, like the ghosts of better times. Kate backed away from her slightly, as though entering the smaller space had her fearful of Flo.

"Kate," Flo said gently. "I think I know why you are so afraid."

"I don't know what you mean, miss," she answered automatically and unconvincingly.

"Ever since I saw you at the Red Lion in Long Compton, you have been terrified of something, or someone," Flo said flatly. "At first, I just wondered if your employee was such a brute that she had made you a nervous wreck. Then, when we discovered you had an invitation, I wondered if that was to do with it. Now I'm pretty sure I know."

Flo folded her arms and stared at her.

"I think you were invited here because you knew Elina Fortesque. In fact, I think you were the one who gave her the information about your employee's relationship with another man."

The girl's head dropped into her hands.

"I didn't know she'd get killed over it," she said, sobbing. "She said there wouldn't be a problem. That Miss Atoll was rich and that all we were doing was taking our bit to help her and make sure she didn't get in trouble."

"How did you meet?" Flo asked, strangely numb now to hearing about this side of her friend.

"Lord Baxter and Miss Atoll were both staying in London when I had an afternoon off. It was a nice day, and I'd gone to the park. I always enjoyed sitting there and watching all the fancy folk from town go about."

She was rambling, but Flo let her continue. At least she was talking now, and she didn't want to interrupt the flow.

"And she just sat next to me on the bench and started talking," she continued. "At first it was all just about the weather and things, and she was so glamorous and pretty and I was just happy she was talking to me and then…" She pulled a handkerchief from her sleeve and blew her nose loudly. "She said she'd seen me with Miss Atoll, that she'd recognised her from the papers and that she knew her type. I asked her what she meant, and she said that Miss Atoll was one that acted posher than most, because she was hiding that she really wasn't posh."

Flo nodded, thinking back to the Elina she had known. She had always been an excellent judge of character. She had enjoyed pointing people out in the cocktail bars and clubs they had frequented and picking apart their mannerisms. Explaining what they showed about their personalities, their lives. Suddenly, Flo could picture Elina as a blackmailer. Someone who knew people, who knew their weaknesses and how to exploit them.

"I knew, you see, about her and that man." Kate gave a shudder at the thought of Henry. "I couldn't not know, could I? They were always meeting up when his lordship was away or when Miss Atoll came into town. She said we could both get some nice money if we just played it right, and no one would get hurt at all as we'd never actually tell his lordship anything—it was just for show!"

Flo nodded. Although, really, she felt that having no intention of going through with black-mail didn't make the actual blackmail part any better.

"Why are you so scared of Henry?" Flo asked.

The girl's round face snapped up to look at her.

"Don't you realise?" she said, her eyes growing wide. "It was him!"

Flo stiffened as she felt a chill run down the back of her neck.

"What was?" she asked, her voice hollow with tension.

"It was him that killed her!" she said in a hoarse whisper, her eyes darting to the door.

Flo took a deep breath through her nostrils, trying to calm her heart, which was now thun-dering in her ears.

"Why do you think Henry killed Elina?" she said.

The girl looked at her as though she were stupid.

"I never knew his name," she said in a rush. "If I'd known his name, I would have told Elina and then she would have known she was in danger! Oh, lord! And it was my fault, all of it!"

She descended into sobs again, and Flo waited

for her to get herself under control as she thought about what the girl had said.

"You didn't know his name, but you'd seen them together," she said softly.

Kate Fielding looked up at her with red-rimmed eyes and nodded.

"You suspected him of having something to do with Elina's death?"

"No, miss," Kate hissed, looking at the door again nervously, "I know he did!" She leaned closer and continued in a low voice. "He came to the house in London after it happened. He'd never done that before, so I knew something was going on. Lord Perciville owns that house and it's all his staff there apart from me. He wouldn't have gone there unless it was something important. I was dying to hear so I..." She looked at Flo with wide, frightened eyes.

"It's OK, Kate," Flo said, "anything you say to me is in confidence."

She swallowed and nodded. "I was listening at the door. They were having an awful row. She was saying he should never have come to the house and that he was going to ruin everything, and then he jumps in and says he already had! He said '*she*' was dead and that he was going to hang for it."

Flo felt the room spin slightly and reached out to steady herself against the wall. Henry Bitten's first thought after Elina's death was that he would hang for her murder. Henry had never been her friend, he had merely been playing a part. He had never been Elina's friend, either. She had simply been his quarry.

"Kate," she said when she could speak again, "when was this in relation to the murder?"

"It was two days after," she said. "I know because when i saw her name in the paper... Well, then I knew. I knew he'd killed her and it was all my fault!"

FORTY

"Rooms all sorted for Mrs Buckley," George said when Flo reentered the drawing room. "The maid's taken her up now."

"Good," Flo said, gratefully taking the drink that Jessie held out to her.

"George," she said, looking him in the eye. "We need to think about whether Henry could have murdered Elina."

He blinked back at her for a moment behind his thick glasses, then glanced at Jessie.

"Oh come on Flo, not Henry."

"Oh come on, George—all that time he spent with us was a lie. He was only there to get closer to Elina, to stop her blackmailing Juliet, no matter what the cost."

He looked down at the floor. "You know, something has been worrying me a little."

"What is it?" she asked, not sure if she wanted to know the answer.

"Last night, when there was all that kerfuffle in the night. Henry said he'd seen me coming out of my room with that poker."

"Yes?" Jessie said encouragingly.

"Well, he couldn't have."

"What do you mean?!" Flo snapped, losing patience with him.

He recoiled slightly, as though she'd reached out to slap him. "Sorry," he said, "I'm not being clear. When I came out of my room, the first thing I did was cross the landing and tried to wake Henry up. When I got to his room, I was about to knock when I realised the door was open a crack. I pushed it open, and he was nowhere to be seen."

"He wasn't in his room," Flo said flatly, the cold and rising dread she felt only intensifying.

"So I decided to go back to my room, and that's where I found you both, and then he suddenly came up behind me saying he'd seen me come out of my room. I didn't know what to make of it at the time, but it was damned odd him saying that."

"He was giving himself an alibi," Flo said softly, causing Jessie to curse next to her.

"He said he saw you come out of your room so that we'd think he'd been in his until that moment.," Jessie said. "When really, he'd been in Hove's room, sorry, Frank Sparks' room, pushing him out of a window!"

"Good lord!" George exclaimed, and slumped back into an armchair.

"When he found Frank Sparks outside," Flo said, her mind working through events, "he might have been checking he was dead, maybe even making sure he was."

"Jeez," Jessie said, "wait, why would he kill Edward Buckley?"

"Maybe it was just a crime of opportunity." Flo shrugged.

"Wait a minute," George said, rising from his chair again and pacing. "He was going through with all this horrible business of allowing his woman to marry another man for money, right?"

"I'll ignore the fact you said 'his woman' in this instance," Jessie said with an eyeball towards Flo, "Go on."

"So he's motivated by money, and also by the

fact that if he killed Elina, he wants to get away with it."

"Right," Jessie agreed.

"So then there's this offer from the mysterious Mr Badala, who brings us here to find Elina's murderer. If we do uncover the murderer, then we get some large inheritance."

"If any of that is actually true," Flo said sceptically.

"Yes, but maybe it is, or at least, maybe Henry thinks it is. Then he can kill two birds with one stone." He paused in his pacing and looked at Flo with a frown. "Sorry, poor choice of words there."

"Just explain what you mean," Flo urged.

"Right, well, if I was in that position, I'd be thinking that I could pin the blame on some poor blighter here for Elina's murder, and then claim part of this inheritance. That way, this Juliet of his can break it off with Lord Perciville and they can live happily ever after and all that."

"And so," Jessie said, nodding, "he kills Edward Buckley thinking he could pin the murder on him and pass it off as either a sleeping draught overdose or a heart problem or something, but then Flo here spotted he'd been suffocated, which threw his plans off."

"I wouldn't be surprised if he tried to frame someone else next," George said.

"Or just murder the lot of us," Jessie added with a grin.

Flo looked at her in shock, before the bizarre nature of the whole situation, mixed with the tension and Jessie's infectious grin, had her suddenly laughing. This caused Jessie to laugh as well, and soon the two of them were in near hysterics. Wiping away their tears, Flo saw a baffled George looking at them both in confusion.

"Sorry George," Flo said, "just the tension, I think."

"Not for me," Jessie said, still laughing. "This is the most alive I think I've ever felt in my life."

Flo's brain was back to thinking through their situation.

They couldn't let Henry know they suspected him of Elina's death, as well as the death of Hove. If he knew they suspected him, he could become desperate. Right now, they were trapped in this gloomy house at the bottom of the valley, and the last thing they needed was a murderer feeling as though he was cornered.

So, what would Henry's next move be? If he

thought he was still unsuspected of being a murderer, he might still hope to lay the blame for Elina's death on someone else, but who? The only outstanding candidates other than himself and Juliet Atoll were the Buckleys, and Edward Buckley was dead. Unless… Unless somehow he could put the blame on Anna Buckley. She was the person with the most access to kill her husband, after all. Maybe Edward Buckley had grown a conscience and had decided to out his wife as Elina's murderer?

She took another sip of her drink and sighed.

"Penny for your thoughts?" George asked.

She looked up at him and smiled. Jessie was busy making yet more drinks at the side table. They were alone.

"It's all just been quite a shock," she said, feeling silly for such a colossal understatement.

"Of course," he said, reaching out his right hand and placing it on her left arm. He rubbed it slightly up and down before removing it and giving her one of his sheepish grins.

"So," Jessie said, returning with three more drinks on a small tray. "What's the big plan?"

"I think it's important we don't let Henry know we suspect him," Flo said. "We need to make him think we blame Edward Buckley for Elina's murder."

"Blame Buckley?" George asked, surprised.

"Yes," Flo said firmly. "I'll make up some nonsense that I made a mistake about how he died. We might even need Anna Buckley to play along if we want to keep things calm until the police get here."

CHAPTER

FORTY-ONE

They found Henry Bitten and Juliet Atoll in the library, both of them falling silent from whatever conversation they had been having. Flo, Jessie and George had decided they would split them up, the women tackling Juliet, George taking Henry.

George's instructions were to play the good buddy with Henry. Put him at ease and carry on as normal. Flo and Jessie, on the other hand, would try to get closer to Juliet. Sympathise with the woman's situation, and see if they could get any more information on Henry's involvement in the deaths.

Flo had feared that the couple would resist being separated, but it was only Henry that seemed unsure when they had insisted on taking Juliet away to 'freshen up.' A phrase that Jessie said men always feared to question in case it revealed an element of the mysterious female which, in their mind, was better left mysterious.

They had been ensconced in Juliet's room for almost an hour now. Her reticence to talk had slowly thawed, and she had fallen into a reflective mood as she now talked between large sips of her gin and tonic.

"Henry and I were like something you read about in a silly novel." She smiled, but then the expression quickly faded to a frown. "Sometimes, it feels as though everything was like that before the war. None of it seems real now." She shuddered slightly, as though trying to shake herself free of her thoughts. "Henry insisted on joining up, lied about his age. I pleaded with him not to go, but he insisted on doing his bit. Still, some part of me always knew he'd come back. Until I heard from his mother that he was missing in action. I think now that the person I used to be died that day."

"He came back, though," Jessie said softly.

"Yes," Juliet smiled, "he came back from the dead to find I'd given up."

"You'd moved on, not given up," Flo said.

Juliet gave a humourless laugh. "I hadn't moved on. I thought about killing myself, you know, but I didn't have the stomach for it. So, I decided that if I was going to live, I might as well do it in luxury. I created a new mysterious back-story for myself and went hunting for an old man with pots of money." She spat the words as though disgusted with herself. Before Flo or Jessie could say anything further, the door to the room opened suddenly.

"Oh!" Juliet's maid squealed as she saw the three of them. "You're here!"

"Of course I'm here," Juliet answered. "Where else would I be?"

Kate Fielding's wide eyes darted between the three of them. "They said that Miss Circle was the murderer, and she'd taken you up to the stone circle!" she said, her hands clasped to her chest.

Jessie laughed loudly. "What on earth are you talking about?!"

Flo's blood ran cold as she rose slowly from the edge of the bed where she had been perched.

"Who said this, Kate?"

"Mr Bitten and Mr Wilson," she answered on the edge of hysteria, "I heard them arguing about it in the hall and then they ran outside! I didn't know what to do," she turned to Juliet, "but I was thinking of you out in that storm, and I thought I'd get you some dry clothes laid out ready for when they brought you back."

Juliet was asking why on earth they had thought that, and Jessie was responding, but Flo wasn't listening to any of it. She was staring at Kate Fielding.

This young woman had been invited here specifically because she had been the one to provide Elina with the information that allowed her to blackmail Juliet. Who, though, had provided the information Elina had required to blackmail the Buckleys? She had not even thought of it until this moment, this moment when two people had headed out into a ferocious storm to rescue Juliet, who was safe and sound beside her. One of those people had lied.

FORTY-TWO

Flo rapped on the door and opened it without waiting for an answer.

"What on earth!" Anna Buckley began, then stopped when she saw the expression on Flo's face. "What is it?"

"The information Elina had on you and your husband. Do you know where she got it?"

"It was all made up, just a pack of lies," she said stiffly.

"Stop!" Flo shouted, making Anna jump and even surprising herself with her ferocity. "This is not the time to protect your bloody reputation. What did Elina have over you, and where did she get the information?"

Anna's face paled. "We never knew," she

answered in a hoarse voice. "Somehow she knew it was Edward who had misused funds, but it wasn't all his fault!" she said, regaining some of her old spirit, "he misused some, but there was so much missing, everything was gone. His partner Cedric must have been deliberately stealing company funds."

Flo closed her eyes as several things started to make sense in a way that she really didn't want them to.

"Did your husband recognise anyone who is here at Standings?" she asked, bracing herself for the answer.

"No," Anna answered confidently, "neither of us had seen anyone here before."

"What's going on? What are you thinking, Flo?" Jessie said from behind her in the hallway.

"I haven't been thinking," Flo said bitterly, "Come on, we need to arm ourselves and get out to the stones before someone else dies."

FORTY-THREE

The rain was no longer the deluge it had been for most of their stay in the gloomy valley. Instead, it had turned into a finer sleet which felt to Flo as though tiny fragments of glass were being ground into her cheeks as she and Jessie made the steep climb towards the standing stones. Each of them held a silver ashtray in their pockets where their hands were stuffed, hastily grabbed as they had left the house. The weighty metal in her hand felt at least mildly reassuring, but the shaking of the hand that held it was not purely from the cold.

"There!" Jessie said, pointing into the gloom ahead of them.

A figure was hunched over at the edge of the

stone circle, walking backwards slowly and dragging something along the ground.

"Come on!" Jessie shouted, and they redoubled their efforts up the slippery slope.

They were only thirty feet from the figure when Flo saw what the intention was. A small stream ran along a crease in the hillside, where it meandered down until it fell sharply off an outcrop of rock that hung over the river some one hundred feet below.

"Jessie, hang back and stay out of sight. It's better if I talk to him alone."

Jessie stared hard at her for a moment, but then nodded. "I won't be far," she said, before darting off towards the stones and out of sight in just a few yards of the driving sleet.

"George!" she shouted, "Stop!"

George Wilson looked up in horror, his eyes wide, although smaller looking without his glasses, which were sticking out of the breast pocket of his coat. His wet blond hair was plastered to his head as he stared at her.

"Flo," he shouted, "it's Henry, he's hurt."

His face darkened as he saw Jessie move up beside her.

"And I suppose Jessie did this?" Flo shouted

at him.

"What?" he said. "Wasn't she with you? Look, Flo, I think there's someone here that is trying to do us all harm."

"Did you work for Cedric Baxter, George?"

The question seemed to hit him like a sledge-hammer. His whole body jerking backwards as his face contorted in a mix of fear and anger.

"Don't listen to this Jessie woman, Flo!" he screamed back at her, "She's poisoned you against me! She's the one we don't know. She turned up here and just invited herself to this bloody house!"

Flo wiped her sleeve across her forehead to clear the rain that was running down her face. "You worked for Baxter," she continued, "and I think you were embezzling money from the company that he and Edward Buckley owned."

"No!" George cried, but his voice was more pleading now than defiant.

"Then, let me guess, Baxter noticed something was wrong? Maybe Edward Buckley was clumsier than you in his attempts to take money out of the company, and that's what Baxter spotted first? Whatever happened, I think he uncovered your theft and so you had to silence him. Luckily for you, you found a way of keeping the money coming in, didn't you? You had Elina, who was desperate for money after her father cut her off. You gave her an opportunity, a way to blackmail the Buckleys. Poor Edward thought he was the only one stealing from the company."

George's entire demeanour had changed now. His arms hung limp at his side, his jaw slack.

"Flo...," he said feebly, one arm rising, palm facing upwards to the dark grey sky.

"Six months," she said, tears now falling to mix with the rain on her cheeks. "Six months ago you killed Elina. You must have thought you had got away with it, so why this?" She gestured at the sombre valley surrounding them. "Why did you lure everyone here? If Edward Buckley was on to you, you could have dealt with him in the same way you did his partner."

"What?!" George roared, "You think I arranged this madness?!" He gestured at the looming hills all around them. The sleet and rain were easing now, leaving the wind to whip about them as they stood on the slope. "Hove was the one. I thought he'd know what the hell was going on, but all I got from him was that, of all people, the butler had hired him, then the man turned out to be nothing but a bloody actor!"

"You pushed him out of his bedroom window," Flo said in more of a statement than a question.

"The butler knew nothing either!" George continued, ranting in frustration now, almost oblivious to the situation. "Said someone hired him anonymously and told him to pick up the money and hire Hove, or whatever he was really called. Someone has orchestrated all of this to set me up!"

"It's not setting you up if you did it, George," Flo said. "Why? Why Elina?" she asked, tears falling down her cheeks despite the fact that a coldness of heart seemed to have crept across her. She no longer felt fear, or even anger. She felt the frozen truth laid before her, and it had made ice in her bones.

"Flo," George said, his features softening again. "All of this was for you, for our future."

"Our future?" Flo replied flatly.

"Yes! When I discovered old Buckland was pilfering money from the company, I saw a chance for me to build a little nest egg of our own. One that would set us up, maybe get us a pleasant cottage by the sea."

Flo kept her features impassive, not wanting to

stop him talking despite a mixture of confusion and revulsion.

He frowned. "Then my boss, Cedric Baxter, suspected something was wrong. I tried to put him on Buckland's trail, but he knew something was off. I had to make sure that I was in the clear and Buckland took the fall, so I arranged things accordingly."

Flo swallowed, forcing herself now to stay impassive. To hear someone she had considered a friend talk so casually of the murder of a man as 'arranging things accordingly' was like some awful nightmare.

"Then, once it was all cleared up, I got another job, but this one didn't quite have the same opportunities, so I arranged things with Elina. That way I could still build for our future, but then it all started to go wrong. Do you know what she was really like, Flo? How scheming and untrustworthy she was? She was a double-crossing little bitch!" he spat with ferocity. "She started blackmailing me! Saying that she would tell you everything and paint me in such a bad way that you would never look at me again. You have to understand, Flo," he pleaded with a shy smile, "I couldn't risk losing you."

Flo held her tongue instead of replying that he had never 'had' her. That the relationship he had built up in his mind, of them settling down in some cottage by the sea, was entirely fictional. The thought that it was this vision of her and their life together that had driven him to this sickened her.

"So," he said, closing his hands together as though in prayer as he looked her in the eye, "we need to think of our future. This," he waved his hand, taking in Henry, who was still prone at his feet, "situation needs dealing with. If we stick together, this Jessie woman can answer for all this and we can move on with our lives."

"Move on with our lives?" Flo repeated in disbelief.

"Yes," he said, stepping over Henry's prone form and moving towards her, "don't you see? We've got an opportunity to start again. Henry has got himself in this spot of bother with the future Lady Perciville. She's going to be worth a pot of money! Why should they be the only ones to bene-fit? We can all live off the money, all four of us. It will be like old times, in a way."

"And what about Juliet's maid? And the butler?"

"Oh," he said with a dismissive snort and wave

of his hand, "you know what these people are like. They'll do anything for a few coppers. We'll give them a little something to keep quiet."

"And Jessie?"

He frowned. "Well, it would be useful to have someone to hang all this on. Easier for us, and really, what do we know about the woman? She seems a strange sort to me."

Flo couldn't believe what she was hearing. The callousness, the indifference to what he had done. His old boss Cedric Baxter, Frank Sparks, who had played the part of the solicitor Hove, Elina. The man in front of her had been the cause of so much horror, yet he treated it as a mere inconvenience. How could he ever think she could love someone like that?

There was a movement from behind George, and it took all her willpower to keep her eyes locked on his. There was only one person it could be—Jessie.

"How could we frame her?" Flo said, knowing she had to play for time. "We don't know she has anything to do with this."

"Oh, that doesn't matter," he said, his entire expression turning hopeful. "We can sort out the details once we've cleared all this mess up."

For a moment, Flo wasn't sure what 'mess' he was referring to, then she realised. He meant the loose ends that would still potentially bring him to justice. He meant Anna Buckley, Juliet Atoll and her maid Kate Fielding. He even meant Jessie, by framing her for murder so that she hanged, and Henry who lay behind him on the wet earth.

Behind him.

Flo moved towards him, her hands out in front of her as though inviting him to take them. He raised his hands, and she darted forward, pushing him hard in the chest. He stepped back where his foot caught on the prone form of Henry, sending him flying backwards, arms windmilling through the air. He landed hard on the wet earth, sliding backwards, as Flo saw Jessie dash forward and swing down an iron-fire poker onto the side of his forehead. There was a dull thud, and George went limp.

CHAPTER

FORTY-FOUR

It was Jessie who had taken over next. Flo had stood there in a daze, as the enormity of events seemed to hit her like a hungry wave, swallowing her whole.

Jessie had, without a hint of embarrassment, removed the still unconscious Henry's belt and bound George's hands behind him, rolling him facedown into the mud to do so. Flo watched dumbly as she cut a new hole in the leather belt with a pocket knife she produced from her coat. She rolled George back and turned instead to Henry, feeling his pulse and then inspecting his head.

"He's going to be fine, Flo," she said before

gently slapping his cheeks, causing his eyes to flutter open. It took a few minutes, but they had finally got him coherent and able to stand. It wasn't long before George had regained consciousness too, though he didn't speak. Instead, he'd kept his head bowed, eyes on the floor as the four of them had unsteadily made their way back to the house.

Before any of them had changed out of their now dripping clothes, George had been further secured to an armchair in the drawing room. They had replaced the belt with a thick string from the kitchen, normally used to bind wax paper packages of meat. He had been left in his wet clothes, but at least positioned by the fire.

Now dry and in fresh clothes, Flo descended the stairs with Jessie, feeling as though she had woken from some terrible nightmare. She headed for the small telephone cupboard at one side of the hallway and asked the operator to put her through to the nearest police station at Chipping Norton. Once connected, an exasperated and gruff male voice answered with a rehearsed line.

"Hello?" Flo said in return, "My name is Florence Hammond. I'm calling from Standings House where a death was reported yesterday."

"A death?" the man replied. "What do you mean a death?"

"A member of the staff of the house called to report the death of a Mr Jonathon Hove, though that wasn't his real name in the end. He was an actor."

"May I remind you that wasting police time is a very serious matter, young lady?" the voice replied.

Flo took a deep breath, trying to remain patient, and put on what she hoped was an innocent 'damsel in distress' voice. "Can you please check if a death has been reported at Standings House, just for me?"

The voice on the other end of the phone cleared his throat. "OK, miss, hold on."

He returned a few moments later. "No one's reported anything to do with Standings House, miss."

Flo pushed back her confusion at this news and made a full report of the goings on at the weather-beaten house. By the time she had finished, the officer on the other end of the line believed her. As she hung up and moved back into the hallway, Jessie and the maid, Kate Fielding, were helping a figure across the room. Each of

THE WILL OF THE STANDING STONES

them was supporting an arm of the butler Stammerthwaite, though Flo was sure that was not his real name. The man looked so different from when they had first arrived at the house, certainly younger. The eye patch was gone, as was the wig of long hair and the fake beard, but he still had the swarthy complexion.

"I'm glad you are awake," Flo said as she met them.

"Thank you, miss," the man said, bowing his head slightly. He looked pale and moved stiffly. Clearly he was conscious, but not in any way recovered.

"I would have thought it would have been better for you to remain in bed?" She looked at Jessie with a raised eyebrow.

"Bearing in mind the man's rapid change of appearance," Jessie said with a half smile, "I thought it better he was where we could all keep an eye on him once Kate here told me he was awake."

"Oh, I think you have the right idea," Flo said, a hardness in her voice that sounded unfamiliar to her own ear. "In any case, I have a few questions for Mr Stammerthwaite myself."

The four of them moved into the drawing

room where Juliet and Anna stood inspecting the wound on the back of Henry's head, an ice pack in Juliet's hand. George sat bound in his armchair by the fire. All four of them looked up as they entered.

"Our transforming butler," Henry said with a mirthless laugh.

"Would you mind if I sat by the fire, miss?" Stammerthwaite asked in a thin voice. Jessie nodded and guided him to the armchair on the right of the fire, facing George, before moving to the sideboard to pour him a large brandy.

"I think it's time you told us who you really are," Flo said, looking the man in the eye, "and how we all came to be here."

The man took the glass Jessie offered him and mumbled thanks before taking a large gulp of the dark liquid.

"It's time," he said, before straightening in his chair, wincing in pain as he did so. He placed the glass on the arm of the chair and reached into his jacket pocket.

Flo held her breath. This was it. This was the moment the man showed them papers that explained exactly how the strange events of this weekend had come about.

Before his hand was out of his jacket, the man

leapt up from his chair and dived towards George. Unable to raise his bound arms in defence, George cried out in alarm, and then pain, as the man known as Fortesque plunged a thin blade into his chest.

F lo dived forward and tried to place her hands over the wound, but she knew it was already too late. George's eyes rolled to her as his bound body jerked and twitched with the shock and pain of the wound.

"I just wanted," he said in a hoarse whisper, "our house by the sea." His eyes opened wide as his body spasmed one last time, his head lolling back.

She rose, looking down at the blood on her shaking hands and turned to Stammerthwaite, who had collapsed onto his knees after the effort of murdering George Wilson. Jessie was pulling him roughly back into the chair. Once she had done so, silence fell over the room. Flo stared at the man in front of her, tears rolling down his cheeks, a sad smile on his face.

"Who are you?" she said at last.

"That can wait," Jessie said, placing an arm around her and guiding her towards the door. "Let's get you cleaned up first."

She guided Flo to the bathroom and left to 'sort things out' in the drawing room. After washing the blood from her hands of someone she had recently counted as a friend, Flo stared at her reflection in the mirror. Her face was pale, revealing very faint freckles that were mostly hidden in her complexion normally. Her hairpin was askew, causing her blonde waves to bulge across the top of her head. She corrected it automatically, as her mind tried to put together some kind of reason for the madness of the past few days. After a few deep breaths and some cold water on her face, she knew she would find no answers here, in the bathroom alone.

She looked at the reflection of the quiet girl, who was more comfortable in the background of things. Was she still that person now? She certainly felt different. As though soft metal had been plunged into a fire and come out hardened. She shook herself free of these thoughts. This wasn't the time for self-reflection. She needed answers.

When she returned to the drawing room, George and the chair they had tied him to were gone. The butler was still seated in the armchair he had been when she'd left, but this time, his hands were tied. Jessie caught her questioning look.

"We took the...," she paused, "we took George into the billiard room."

Flo nodded and looked around at what was left of their group. Anna Buckley was sitting on a high-backed chair near the drinks cabinet, her face ashen as she clutched a gin and tonic. Juliet Atoll and Henry Bitten were sitting together. Juliet perched on the arm of the chair, still holding the ice bag to Henry's head. Juliet's maid, Kate Fielding, was there too, hovering near the door, looking nervous.

Flo realised that they all seemed to be waiting for her to do something. Even Jessie, who Flo had already come to realise enjoyed being the centre of attention, was looking at her now.

She took a deep breath and moved in front of the man tied before the fireplace.

His face was calm. He showed no sign of anger,

worry, or even discomfort at being tied to a chair and surrounded by unfriendly eyes. Flo continued where she had left off.

"Who are you?" she said in a loud, clear voice.

The man smiled. "I must thank you Miss Hammond," he said, his voice a deep, rich bass. His accent, English, with a hint of something more exotic.

"Thank me?" Flo asked.

"For being a genuine friend to my daughter," he replied.

Flo felt the room swim, and she closed her eyes. When she opened them again, she was gripping onto the mantlepiece with her left hand to steady herself, and Jessie had moved towards her to help.

"I'm OK," she said to her quietly, and Jessie nodded, but stayed by her side.

"You're Elina's father," she said, turning back to the man, who nodded his agreement.

"It was you who arranged all this," she said, gesturing around them at the house. He nodded again.

"My daughter and I may not have seen eye-to-eye on everything," he said, his voice cracking slightly, "but she was everything to me. I wrote to her every day; every day I hoped she'd change her mind and come back to me."

"You'd cut her off financially," Flo said, realising with a jolt that she meant that to hurt. She was angry.

"I did." He nodded sadly. "I thought it might force her to wake up, to realise that she needed me." He snorted in disgust. "I was a fool."

"Did you know she was blackmailing people?" Flo asked.

He shook his head. "Not until," he paused and closed his eyes, "not until after I heard she had died. I came here straight away on the first ship I could get on. My business operates out of India, you see."

Flo nodded.

"When I arrived in London, I went through what belongings there were of hers. It made me realise how far I had let her fall," he said bitterly. "She had nothing but a few outfits, a diary and a notebook that showed how far she had really gone to survive financially without my support."

"Blackmail," Flo said quietly.

He nodded. "I knew then why she had been killed. Someone in that book was responsible. I spent the next few months setting up this house and arranging a reason for you all to gather here."

"Mr Badala," Flo said, "that name." She shook her head. "Something about it struck me from the start, something I'd read."

He gave a mirthless smile. "In Hindi, it means revenge. That was my purpose here. I wanted the person who had killed my daughter to die." His eyes were hard circles of pain, but suddenly softened and a tear rolled down his cheek. "I never meant for anyone else to die," he mumbled.

"Frank Sparkes," Flo said. "You hired him to play the part of a solicitor, Hove."

Fortesque nodded. "He knew nothing about what was really going on. He damn near ran out of here when he read the letter I gave him on the standing stones. I never thought that he would be in danger. He knew nothing!"

"But George Wilson didn't know that," Flo said. "He tried to get information out of the only person here who seemed to know what was going on, and Frank Sparkes ended up falling from his bedroom window."

"I didn't mean for that to happen," Fortesque said, his chin dropping to his chest. "I just wanted Elina's killer to pay."

FORTY-SIX

F lo gazed out of the window at the train station platform outside. The steam from the train that had just pulled in whirled and coated the view in swirling whites and greys, as though the world were out of focus.

She looked up as the bell on the café door gave its soft tinkle. Jessie Circle stood framed in the doorway, her grey eyes scanning the small space until they came to rest on hers. Flo smiled with genuine affection.

"How are you holding up?" Jessie said as she reached her table and they embraced.

"Not too bad," Flo said, causing Jessie to pull back and inspect her with a critical, slightly disbelieving look.

"Well, I don't believe you, but the fact that you're able to lie about it tells me you're OK."

She ordered herself a coffee and the two of them sat in silence for a while, occasionally looking at the large clock that hung on the far wall. When it reached eleven o'clock, Flo closed her eyes and took a deep breath.

"It's over," she breathed, and Jessie reached across the table to take her hands in hers, saying nothing.

"Tell me," Flo said. "Was it really a coincidence that you were there in that inn when all of this began?"

Jessie pulled her hands away, leaned back and smiled.

"Do you know, Flo? I think you are one of the most intelligent people I've ever met."

"Is your plan to flatter me into forgetting the question?" Flo smiled, making Jessie laugh.

"Do you know," Jessie said with a grin, "I've realised that I'd been missing something I didn't even know I needed."

"And what's that?"

"A partner in crime, figuratively speaking, of course."

"Go on," Flo said, sipping at her tea.

"I've already told you I'm lucky enough to not need to worry about money, but that presents its own problems."

"Such as?"

"Boredom," Jessie said, "plain and simple boredom. After my ward died and I inherited, I found that the days were long and the nights longer. Oh, I spent a good deal of time living the high life, but pretty soon life seemed to fade into a bland series of repeating days."

"So, what did you do?"

"I decided that I would seek out excitement—I would use my money to look for possibilities."

"Possibilities? What does that mean?"

"I have a number of people I have reached out to in order to pass over any interesting bits of information, even advertised in newspapers. Anything curious that seems out of the ordinary."

"That seems vague..."

"It is rather," Jessie agreed. "I have to admit that ninety-nine percent of this information either turns out to be of a completely ordinary nature, or is simply untrue gossip."

"And is that what happened with Standings House? Someone alerted you to what was going to happen there that weekend?"

Jessie laughed. "That's just it, Standings was a complete accident. I was just in the area sightseeing, and who should turn up in the sleepy village inn I'm staying at, but a whole cast of characters called to stay at a country house for a will reading. I think it must have been fate somehow."

Flo shook her head in amazement "I'd imagine that weekend was enough to put you off your quest for finding interesting quirks of life."

"Not at all!" Jessie replied with glee. "This was the first time the enterprise had been worthwhile!" She leaned forward and lowered her voice. "We managed to uncover your friend's killer."

"Yes," Flo answered flatly, "but not bring him to justice."

Jessie shrugged. "Hangman's noose isn't much different than a vengeful father's blade."

"It's all the difference in the world," Flo said quietly, before she shook off her melancholy and turned back to the interesting case of Jessie Circle.

"What other interesting scenes of life have you uncovered with this hobby of yours?"

The smile on Jessie's lips faded, and Flo saw an expression on the young woman's face she had not seen in the few weeks she had known her. A mix of fear and sadness.

"Oh, I've had some interesting times, that's for sure. Got in with a bad lot for a while." She cleared her throat and her smile returned. "I'm afraid I bit off rather more than I could chew for a while. I decided some time across the pond might be in order."

"Excuse me?"

Flo turned to see a tall man in a dark suit peering down at her.

"Are you Miss Flo Hammond?"

"I am."

"I realise this is rather unusual, but I represent the law firm of Holder and Bailey, and I have been instructed to deliver this to you at this time. Our details are enclosed. We expect to hear from you shortly." He gave a curt bow, turned, and left.

"What on earth?" Flo said, looking at Jessie, who shrugged back.

"I've no idea. You'd best open it."

Flo turned the thick envelope over in her hands before breaking the seal and pulling the papers from it. There was a thick stack of what looked like legal documents, on top of which was a handwritten letter.

· · ·

Dear Florence,

I do not regret my last action, I only regret the additional loss of life that resulted from it. One thing is clear to me, though, you were a loyal friend to Elina, even after her death. When I created my trap at Standings House, I promised that the person who uncovered Elina's murderer would inherit a vast fortune. I'm not sure if my estate could be vast, but it is at least substantial. I have no family. Elina was my world, my universe. It is fitting, and satisfying to me that someone who was there for her when I wasn't should benefit in her place. I have arranged a substantial amount for the family of Frank Sparks. This will not absolve me of his death, but it is all I can do.

The rest, will go to you.

I have arranged for this letter to be delivered after the allotted time for my hanging. Everything is in place.

All I ask is that you never forget Elina, and that you honour her in some way by making your own life a success. A tribute to what could have been for my dear Elina.

Life is nothing without love, and I go to my end in peace, knowing I have none left in this world.

Yours faithfully,

JOHN FORTESQUE.

EPILOGUE

Flo smiled as she looked down at her copy of The Evening Standard newspaper.

"I can't believe it," she said with a laugh, "two whole pages!"

"That's not all," Jessie said, leaning over and pointing to the end of the article with her finger.

Flo took a sharp intake of breath. There, at the end of the article was her real name. Florence Hammond.

"But...how?!" She said, looking up at Jessie who laughed, her head tipping backwards.

"I made a small advertising contribution on the strict instruction that you would be rightfully named for the write up of what happened at Standings house."

"An advertising contribution? What on earth would you be advertising?"

Jessie smiled and something about it had Flo's heart beating slightly quicker. Jessie's finger moved to a box in the top right of the article Flo hadn't noticed. It read...

Hammond & Circle - Investigators

As discreet or as public as you wish, no mystery too big, small or dangerous.

For when only a woman's wiles will do

Flo turned to Jessie with a look of horror.
"Oh goodness Jessie what have you done?!"
Jessie grinned back at her.
"Hopefully, starting our next adventure."

AFTERWORD

In writing this series, I borrow from places and events in the real world, but every regarding the story is fiction.

Long Compton is indeed a real village in the Cotswolds of England, as is the Red Lion pub that resides there (excellent roast dinners if you're ever in the area!).

Nearby are some of the oldest stone circles in Britain, the Rollright Stones. They are said to have been a king and his men, turned to stone by a witch.

You can read more about this fascinating stone circle here: www.rollrightstones.co.uk

More from AG Barnett

Brock & Poole Mysteries

An Occupied Grave

A Staged Death

When The Party Died

Murder in a Watched Room

The Final Game

The Mary Blake Mysteries

An Invitation to Murder

A Death at Dinner

Lightning Strikes Twice

The Hammond & Circle Mysteries

The Will of the Standing Stones

FREE BOOK

Claim your free book by signing up to AG Barnett's mailing list at agbarnett.com

Printed in Great Britain
by Amazon